Girl
at the
Crossing
A NOVEL

Blaine M. Yorgason

MILLENNIAL PRESS
Salt Lake City, Utah

ISBN 1-930980-66-3

First Printing, 2002

Lithographed in the United States of America
MILLENNIAL PRESS
Salt Lake City, Utah

For additional copies, please contact Millennial Press
at 1-800-217-4881.

Appreciation

May I express grateful appreciation to Clive and Ann Payne of St. Columb, Cornwall, U.K., for their time, their energy, their knowledge, their wisdom, and their willingness to drive all over the bluebell-covered hills and vales, shores and moors of Cornwall, rather than suffer ignominious disaster due to my America-trained driving. More importantly, I thank them for their delightful humor, for I believe we laughed for nine days straight as we sought out the geographical elements of this project.

Clive took elocution classes as a child, and we never tired of listening to he and Ann work wonders with the English language. Neither did we tire of listening to their stories, personal histories, and experiences. These I recorded as they spoke them, and have since transcribed many of them to the pages of this book. With all my heart I have endeavored to portray the Paynes as they really are—as my wife Kathy, daughter Tami and I came to know and to love them.

I have done the same with David and Jeanette Fellick—wonderful innkeepers and delightful hosts—who made our stay at their lovely Granite Henge Bungalows at Trelawne Cross in Looe an unforgettably sweet experience.

I express appreciation to my daughter, Tami Bestenlehner, who accompanied her mother and me specifically so she could watch over and assist her mother during the hours and days when I would not be around. I also thank her husband, David, and her children, Jessa, Mitchell, Halli, Andrew, and Christopher (with whom she was pregnant at the time) for their great sacrifice in the cause.

Finally, I express deep affection to Don and Kathleen Lind, dear friends from America who sacrificed almost all in their kind and thoughtful willingness to show us London. And what a remarkable way they chose to introduce us to the hazards of British intersections and roundabouts....

For Trav—
It's coming, I assure you!

Some have called him a throwback to an earlier time, or a man born a century or more too late. From time to time even he's thought the same. According to him, it's because there are so few like him, and he most always feels out of place. At least that's what he's told me. I believe him, too, because whatever else might be said about Wilford Abbott, the truth's as dear to him as his sweet mother's love. Which is what makes the last story he told me the more remarkable. Unlikely as it sounded, knowing Wilf as I do, I knew it had to be the truth.

Now, Wilf's a traveling man, and I don't know any better way to put it. He's never married, never settled down in one place. Since getting his growth he's been on the go, exploring new places and poking around where few others would even think to look. At one time or another he's been all the way from Alaska to the bottom of South America and a good many places in between, so I suppose it's natural he'd have an itch to try somewhere else.

One other thing before I start. Wilf has some mighty definite opinions about what's just and right. He has no patience with rudeness and injustice, and there's no breath of fear in him when he takes a stand against it. Stacked odds don't mean a lick to Wilf Abbott! Maybe that's because he's the product of a close family and a hardworking, back-country Arizona ranch; I don't know. What I do know, is that this fearless need to confront injustice is what seems to have led him into that story I was telling you about....

Chapter One

*I*t wasn't even hard. In fact, Wilf Abbott hardly had to push himself away from the station-house wall. When the two strange-looking young thugs came slouching off the Looe to Liskard train that afternoon, saw the older couple waiting to board, and snatched the woman's purse, they made their escape straight toward him along the narrow concrete platform. Timing it without difficulty, Wilf merely rolled his wheeled luggage into their path, tripping the first into the second and sending them both sprawling onto the ancient concrete. Then he chuckled.

"Boys, boys, boys," he chided, "you shouldn't have done that. No, sir, you really shouldn't have!"

Before either of the two could scramble to his feet, Wilf was between them, the pointed toe of his scuffed old boot kicking one in the midsection and then his arched instep landing squarely over the scrawny wrist of the other, the youth who had snatched the woman's purse.

"Let it go," he suggested amiably enough while the woman and her husband watched in surprised amazement. Sixty seconds had not passed since the purse had been grabbed, and already the two thieves were down and their unknown benefactor had the situation in hand.

"I said, let it go!" Wilf's voice, still quiet, suddenly had an edge, and when he twisted and pushed his boot, grinding the youth's wrist against the rough cement, the pock-faced older of the two young men shrieked and let go of the purse.

"Thank you kindly." Wilf scooped up the purse and stepped back, his eyes not leaving the two Brits which, now that he looked at them a little more closely, he could see were most likely brothers. Strange and almost alien-appearing, yes, but brothers nonetheless. Both young men had ears pierced with dozens of rings and studs; they sported eyebrow and nose rings, the rings and studs in their lips and tongues looked positively painful; their sallow complexions, ridiculous clothes, outlandishly orange and green colored and spiky coiffed hair, and even their terrible looking teeth, were as repulsive as anything Wilf had ever seen. And though he had felled them both because of the stolen purse, Wilf found himself wanting nothing more than to burst out laughing while he walked away. Never in his life had he seen anything so ridiculous, so pathetically repulsive!

Of course, he admitted candidly, they might be thinking the same of him. Six feet tall and trim to the point of looking gaunt, Wilf kept what hair he had left cropped close. Dressed in faded jeans, his old but favorite cowboy boots, and a brown flannel shirt ordered from a mail-order catalogue by his older sister Annie, he probably looked even more out of place than they did. Looked, and felt, too, he thought wryly, for this was England, and he was a mighty long way from his home in Arizona.

With a muttered curse the brother who had actually grabbed the purse—Orange-hair—was back on his feet, grimacing and rubbing his wrist where the skin had been scraped off. The other—Green-hair—who was still trying to get his breath, was upright and stumbling to the side of his ailing brother.

Thinking they had had enough, Wilf picked up the handle to his luggage, turned, and walked to the woman who had lost the purse. "Here you go, ma'am." He smiled to reassure her. "Sorry you had to see all that violence—"

The look in the woman's eyes, as she stared past Wilf, warned him, and he turned to see the green-haired brother starting in his direction with an open switchblade knife in his hand.

"Would you mind watching my luggage, please?" he asked the couple, and without waiting for an answer, he turned and strode back to meet the advancing sibling hoodlums. He'd had no formal training against such a weapon, he knew, but he wasn't going to sit by while they went after the elderly woman's purse again. Neither was he about to turn tail and run from these miserable punks—knife or no knife!

"Cheeky bird, ain't she," the orange-haired older brother sneered as he also whipped open his knife and stooped into a ridiculous crouch, his attention now on Wilf.

It was a statement, not a question, though what it meant Wilf had no idea. "Excuse me?" he asked softly, not for an instant taking his eyes from the two waving knives.

"Ahh, the bloke's a Yank, is he?" The bizarre-looking young man grinned knowingly as he moved his blade in a wide, slow circle. "The dove what had the handbag, the one you'll soon be cut for—cheeky. Saucy. But she's dicey, too, mate. Risky. The old general there looks like he's her bloke, so she'll come dear if you plan to do much snogging in the dark with her."

"Snogging?" Wilf questioned while the younger brother stopped his moaning to cackle at the foul humor.

The Brit's leering grin grew wider. "Snogging means kissing and cuddling, mate. You know. What all birds is good for, young or old alike, at least if a bloke's a randy and half twee Yank."

"Half twee, huh." The vulgar sense of what was being said was now becoming clear, and Wilf could feel the ire rising within him.

"Righto," the much-pierced young man replied disgustedly as he shifted his dirty, sandled feet in preparation for what Wilf felt would be a lunge. "Crazy innocent. Which from the looks of things, Joe Bloggs, you are."

"I'm sorry," Wilf murmured quietly as he prepared himself, "but that isn't my name."

"It is if I want it to be," the young man sneered as his crouch deepened and his fingers gripped the knife more tightly.

"I wouldn't do that," Wilf cautioned as the other brother also lowered himself into a crouch. "Either of you."

"Why not?" the older youth snapped, and with a hard lunge he thrust his knife at Wilf's abdomen.

Deftly the young American stepped back, throwing the charger off balance. Reaching in, he slapped the knife hand to the side, instantly brought his hand back hard across the startled youth's sallow face, turning him halfway around and accidentally ripping two rings from his nose with the edge of his high school ring. In far less time than it takes to tell it, he then kicked the sharp toe of his boot against the troublemaker's ankle and watched as he sprawled in blood and pain onto the cracked concrete of the platform, his knife skittering off against the station wall.

"Because at least in America that's assault," Wilf smiled down at the groaning youth, who was wailing and holding his torn and bleeding nose in both cupped hands, "which is far more serious than simple theft."

"I'll get you for that, Joe Bloggs!" the surprised but still upright younger brother yelped as he, too, prepared to lunge.

"I don't think so," Wilf grinned even more widely as he stepped back. "It's too bad, though, with all that piercing your head's been through, nobody thought to insert a brain."

"What? You dirty yob, nobody talks to the Penryn brothers that way—"

"Then what about this way?" a voice questioned from directly behind the young man. "Neville Penryn, you're under arrest! The same for you, Petroc." And before either young man could react, a uniformed police officer had taken away Neville's knife and was deftly slipping handcuffs onto his wrists.

"I tried to warn you fellows," Wilf said as he nodded greetings to the officer. "John Law's been sitting over there in his car the past fifteen minutes. He saw the whole thing!"

"Waiting for these two Penryn yobs, as a matter-of-fact," the policeman grunted as he struggled with the youth he had just cuffed. "They got in a bit of trouble down in Looe before they jumped the train this afternoon, and I got the ring. And you were right, young fellow. Assault is a great deal more serious than petty theft—"

Suddenly the one with the torn and bloody nose—Petroc—started to his feet. But before he was even half upright the reed-thin elderly man, Wilf was certain now he was the husband of the woman who had lost the purse, was there pushing him back to the platform.

"Here, here," he soothed as he pushed his bony knees into the youth's back and held his face to the concrete with both his hands. "You lie still, now. Lovely. That's the good little fellow—"

"You're hurting me!" the youth wailed as he writhed under the old man's knees.

"Yes, I should hope so. Such are the wages of grabbing handbags from sweet little things like my Ann!"

"Thank you, both of you," the officer said as he held the one youth by the cuffs while tossing Wilf another pair. "I do appreciate the assist."

"Here, sir," Wilf grinned at the elderly man as he took one of the pinned-down youth's arms and slipped on the cuffs, "before you hurt the poor kid too badly."

"And well I might," the man smiled back as he relaxed. "War-time training, you know. And lightning-fast reflexes. They say neither goes away!"

"Well, they certainly haven't gone far from you." Carefully Wilf helped the old soldier to his feet. He wasn't sure if the man was being serious or not, but from the twinkle in his eye, Wilf concluded that he was poking a bit of fun.

"Now it's your turn," Wilf grunted as he leaned down and pulled the still-moaning Petroc upright by the cuffs. "And except for your nostril you aren't that hurt, so stop your fool caterwauling!"

Moments later, the two would-be thieves were off in the rear seat of the police vehicle, the thankful woman had her purse, and she, her still animated husband, and lastly Wilford Abbott—now being proclaimed a hero by both elderly Brits—were boarding the single-car train for the thirty-five minute journey to Looe.

If what happened to him in England is to make any sense, another thing about Wilf Abbott I should probably mention is that he's a friendly sort, quick to smile and laugh. As a result, people just naturally gravitate to him. Ask any of his brothers or sisters who their favorite sibling is, and each one will point to him. And late at night when he gets on the phone to complain about a mistake on some bill or having to pay what he thinks is too much interest on a credit card, he wears down the poor girls who usually take his calls, until after maybe an hour he's not only got what he wanted in the first place, but they're calling him 'Wilf dear' and dropping hints so maybe he'll call them back for another reason altogether.

Funny thing is, instead of reveling in such popularity, he'd most times rather be alone, pondering life's mysteries and keeping his eyes on the far horizon. It isn't that he has answers nobody else has. It's just that he likes pondering the questions....

Chapter Two

"Wilford Abbott, I must say, you're every woman's dream of a dashing hero! Tall, fine looking—isn't he a handsome one, Clive?"

"He's lovely, all right," Clive Payne responded without any trace of sarcasm in his voice, though again Wilf thought the twinkle in his eyes had given him away.

"Did you learn to fight like that in the service?"

"You mean the military?" Wilf responded with a grin. "No, older brothers."

"Ahh," the elderly man nodded with understanding. "Very good. Absolutely lovely."

Wilf shifted nervously, wishing there was some way he could have remained alone. Not that these weren't good people, for they seemed nice enough and were extremely friendly. Their names were Payne—Clive and Ann—and they would have none of his sitting alone, not now that he had rescued Ann's handbag from the two thieves. Worse, it also turned out they were the talkative type, and so Wilf was resigned to having no peace until they were off the train in Looe and he was once again free to explore the English countryside alone.

Beneath their feet the wheels of the slow-moving, one-car train clattered along the track, making a rhythm of an altogether different sort from the fast clipping of the train he had taken westward out of London's Victoria Station early that morning. That train had sped right along, delighting him with its speed as he had assimilated the views from its windows to begin forming for himself a mental picture of England. But now, he thought ruefully, he'd never have a chance to look outside, much less assimilate anything.

"Is this your first time in merry olde England?" Ann Payne asked with a sweet smile.

Wilf nodded. "First time in England or anywhere else this side of the Atlantic."

"Are you on holiday, then? Or visiting family?"

"I have no family here, but if holiday means the same as vacation, then I guess that's why I'm in England. I met a girl a year or so back who told me Great Britain was a place I had to see and that Cornwall was where to start. So, here I am."

"Alone?"

Wilf grinned. "I've been alone so long, Mrs. Payne—"

"Please call me Ann, and call Clive by his given name, too." Gently the woman smiled. "Neither of us would know to respond otherwise."

"Very well, Ann, I don't even think of it as being alone. What sort of a train is this, anyway?"

"Oh, he likes our quaint transportation," Clive smiled at Ann, his humorous sarcasm now less hidden. "You don't care for a single-car train with a driver's compartment at each end?"

"It's intriguing; I'll say that."

"Well put," Ann laughed. "Actually, Wilford, this is an old commercial line that's been converted to a thirty-five minute scenic tour. I'm certain we haven't given you a chance to notice, but when we departed from Liskeard we went back under the viaduct carrying the main line from Plymouth and London down to Falmouth and Penzance, and we are now performing a large loop that will end at a tiny spot called Coombe Junction. Coombe means narrow valley, by the by. There the train will stop, the engineer will throw the manual switch and move to the other end of our car, and the next thing you know he will be spiriting our quaint little train other end first down the lovely East Looe River to Looe, where the river flows into the English Channel."

Glancing out the window, Wilf saw brilliant green pastures with fields of bluebells covering the steep Cornish hillsides, with ivy-covered walls marching almost willy-nilly up and down and back and forth across them, seeming almost frantic in their efforts to divide one field from another. And all the while, the train was moving so slowly it was not even frightening the various sorts of livestock cropping grass along its tracks.

Through open pastures and then dark and slightly mysterious woods, the single coach continued, tree branches bumping and brushing the windows like soft green brooms. Gradually Wilf realized how much he was actually enjoying the slow-moving ride. For the moment, Clive and Ann Payne seemed content to enjoy it too, and so with an inner sigh he settled back to more thoroughly take it all in.

At Coombe Junction, he watched with interest as the engineer stepped out, threw the heavy switch, then climbed back aboard and started the train in the other direction. The East Looe River, now that he could see bits of it through the lush foilage, was tiny—not much more than an Arizona irrigation ditch—and it was choked with trees, rocks, and hummocks of bright green grass. It was—

"We'll be coming up to our first real stop in a moment or so," Ann suddenly declared, her speech so rapid Wilf found it difficult to follow. "It's a tiny village called St. Keynes."

"Named after one of our ancient and little-known Celtic saints," Clive added. "Though because of his gifted well, this saint might be a bit better known."

"His gifted well?"

"Yes, and a lovely one it is." Clive smiled. "The reported virtue of the water is this, that, whether husband or wife comes first to drink of the water, they get the mastery of their marriage. In a ballad by a fellow named Southby, a man just after his wedding came to take a drink so he would be Master for Life. Unfortunately, at least for him, his wife had been the first to prove her mettle. Would you care to hear the line?"

Learning not to be surprised by this elderly British gentleman, who constantly reminded him of the military-oriented grandfather character who flew his outhouse around in the Disney movie, "Chitty Chitty Bang Bang," Wilf nodded.

"Very well. The ballad concludes:

> I hastened, as soon as the wedding was done,
> And left my Wife in the porch;
> But i' faith she had been wiser than me,
> For she took a bottle to church.

Wilf was still chuckling when Ann stopped him with the one question he hated worse than any other.

"And aren't you married, Wilford?" she asked, looking sad in the same way all his aunts looked sad whenever the subject of his seemingly eternal single status was brought up.

"No, and never have been," Wilf responded, doing his best to keep the irritation out of his voice. Marriage! How he was tired of the subject! Truthfully, now that he was thirty- four and balding quite severely, he had come to the natural conclusion that the closest he would ever come to a wedding was in the"best man" role he had played for all his brothers and erstwhile best friends. Let all of them, like the fellow Clive had described at the well of St. Keynes, be ruled by the wiles of women. For him it was sufficiently joyful to remain free, to have no woman think herself his master. Yet in moments of introspection, Wilf had been forced to admit, if only to himself, that within him there existed a certain loneliness that was proving ever more troublesome—ever more difficult to ignore.

"So," Wilford said, changing the subject, "you fought in the war?"

Clive Payne's eyes twinkled as though this were some great joke, and Wilf had the uncomfortable feeling that the old man knew exactly what he was about. Nevertheless, he allowed himself to be led along.

"Yes, Wilford, I served God and King in World War II. Of course you know that the war was a great deal more threatening here than it was in the States, because, of course, the Germans were only thirty miles across the Channel from us. For years the Nazis had us under heavy bombardment —"

"That's right!" Abruptly Wilf remembered a British history class he had taken years before. "The Germans used experimental rockets on you folks."

"They did," Ann agreed, "the V-1 flying bombs and the V-2 rockets, which had a devastating effect on London and other areas where they happened to hit. But we were also bombed day and night by the *Luftwaffe*, the Nazi air force. They came in wave after wave, hundreds and even thousands of them, and it was terrifying when the air-raid sirens signalled their coming. In fact, the *Luftwaffe* are what destroyed both Plymouth and Exeter in Devon, and also did some damage here in Cornwall."

"Of course," Clive continued, taking over the account, "I wasn't here for most of that. I was serving in—"

"Clive, all this must be very boring to poor Wilford."

"No," Wilf exclaimed, feeling unaccountably sincere, for he did love history. "I'd like to hear!"

Clive smiled brightly at his wife. "There, my dear. You see? I hope that satisfies you. I'll tell young Wilford my part, and then if he still wishes to hear, you may tell him yours."

"Oh, very well, though I doubt our ride will be of sufficient length for half of your stories. But go to it, if that is what you wish."

Wilf smiled as he listened to the gentle banter that denoted the couple's obvious love for each other. Clive and Ann had accents like all Brits, but unlike the young men at the station, it was pleasant listening to them. Rarely did either of these two use a word he did not understand. Apparently, he thought, British youth had the same troubling tendency as American youth, forever perverting the language to their own narrow interpretations and points of view.

"In 1937, Wilford, I joined the Territorial Cavalry, which later became the Nottinghamshire Yeomanry or Sherwood

Rangers. I wasn't yet even shaving on a regular basis, of course, but I felt it my duty."

"We all felt to do our duty," Ann added softly.

"Quite right. In 1939, I was ordered to bring my sabre and spurs and proceed to barracks in Newark. Maneuvers took place in the Yorkshire Dales, where as a mounted machine gunner with a pack horse, I had two animals to care for—double mucking out, cleaning, and feeding, you understand.

"After a few weeks I was assigned to the 6th Cavalry Brigade and moved south with 650 horses and cavalrymen to sail to France. In France, we went by train to Marseilles and then by ship to Haifa—then part of Palestine. Assigned to the Royal Scots Greys, I participated in various skirmishes and forays into the hills bordering Syria."

"Syria? In World War II?"

"Quite right. The local population apparently had Nazi leanings, for they made things a bit hot for us from time to time. In 1941, our regiment gave up horses and was mechanized, and we were then sent to Libya. Joining the coastal defence artillery, we saw a great deal of action and had some rather frightening moments. Then across the desert we drove our mechanized units to Tobruk. There a siege by German and Italian armies under Rommel lasted six months, bringing about terrible hardship and frequently driving us into caves for shelter from the bombardment. Tanks came into our lives in 1942 when we were ready for Alamein and our thrust against General Rommel. When Tobruk was finally relieved, I was shipped out on a Royal Navy destroyer, and in December of 1943 I was returned to England, where I engaged in top-secret duties preparatory to D-Day, which was on 6 June, 1944. On that date, the main force of my regiment attacked Normandy at Arromanches with floating tanks, and I believe we contributed significantly to the success of the invasion."

"Clive's being a bit modest," Ann stated brightly. "After all, he was a true hero, both in Europe and in Africa."

"Is that right?" To his surprise, Wilf was very much enjoying himself—and the Paynes.

"If I was a hero," Clive grumbled, "it was no more than any of the others—"

"Oh, be still, darling. Modesty ill becomes you." Ann then turned to Wilf. "If we were at home, Wilford dear, I would show you an entire chest full of medals and commendations. One of the latter, addressed to Warrant Sergeant Clive Banfield Payne, Notts Yeomanry, reads, and I quote: 'It has been brought to my notice that you have performed outstanding good service and shown great devotion to duty during the campaign in Northwest Europe. I award you this certificate as a token of my appreciation,' and so on. It is signed by B.L. Montgomery, Field Marshall, Commander-in-Chief, 21st Army Group."

"Impressive. You've memorized it?"

"Yes," Ann smiled, "given fifty plus years, it isn't that difficult. He has another commendation that's even more impressive, when he was awarded the MBE (Military Division) for gallant and distinguished service in the Middle East and Northwest Europe. On that commendation, King George VI wrote: 'I greatly regret that I am unable to give you personally the award which you have so well earned. I now send it to you with my congratulations and best wishes for your future happiness.' It is signed George R., who of course was George VI, King of England."

"No kidding?" Wilf was now being absolutely sincere. "Imagine that. The King of England! You really are a hero, Clive! I feel honored just knowing you."

"And well you should," Clive replied with his characteristically good-humored sarcasm. "Unfortunately we national heroes are dying off like flies and have been for sixty years and more. I'm one of the few to worship that's still left alive."

"Clive Banfield Payne!"

Again Wilf chuckled at the man's droll humor. "And I do, Clive. Devoutly. But I have to tell you, in spite of your regal bearing and your wonderful mustache, of which I have never seen the like, you seem to have aged much faster than Ann."

"That's because he started many years before me," Ann replied brightly. "He's a good eighty, Wilford, while I'm hardly sixty-nine."

"You're eighty, Clive? I would never have guessed!"

"My dear boy, you may pay me such compliments any time you wish! Though if the truth were known, I now use my morning lumbago as a reminder that I'm still in the land of the living."

"I have those aches and pains," Wilf grinned, "and I'm hardly eighty. But let's see. If you're a young sixty-nine, Ann, and I mean *very* young, that means you were either a very young child bride, or you met Clive after the war."

Ann laughed delightedly. "Both, actually. And I must say that you are not only dashingly handsome, Wilford, but truly charming! Thank you!"

Wilf nodded with a soft smile.

"At seventeen, I left school, met Clive, knew in an instant that we were meant for each other, and so I became wife to an old man of almost thirty. But I must say that Clive was a dashing figure of a man despite his age, and I've never considered myself anything but lucky to have got him."

"And I to have let her do it," Clive added with his sly grin.

Wilf did not look at Ann, though it was her to whom he was speaking. "You say you knew in an instant that you and Clive were meant for each other?" he asked, trying to keep his voice steady. "May...I ask how you knew? I mean, was there some sort of sign or something?"

"Like Cinderella's glass slipper?" Ann laughed easily. "No, Wilford, there was no great sign, though I do believe the moment was miraculous—a true gift from God in heaven. It was a wonderful feeling, you see, a sort of peaceful certainty that I would be well-loved by this man for the rest of forever. Isn't that what you felt, Clive?"

"That, or perhaps a severe case of indigestion," Clive responded with a sly wink.

"Clive, can't you see that Wilford is being serious?"

"Yes, yes, of course." Clive shifted uneasily, and Wilf sensed that the old soldier's training in keeping a stiff upper lip was making this self-revelation somewhat unpleasant. "It was much the same for me," the elderly hero finally acknowledged. "I'd never looked upon such beauty in my life, and I never wanted the view of her to go away. Thankfully, she has not."

"So, you both sensed something that was at least out of the ordinary if not actually extraordinary." It was meant as a statement, not a question, and now Wilf watched their faces carefully.

"Quite right. Very much so."

"And for me it was *very* extraordinary," Ann declared. "But, may I ask why you are so concerned with this?"

Slowly Wilf let out his breath. "No reason, really." He grinned disarmingly. "Only, Mom used to tell me the same thing—that I would know."

"And you have not?"

"Well," Wilf chuckled, "that depends. I know, for instance, that I've never met anyone I felt like marrying."

Ann chuckled. "That isn't what I meant, Wilford, and I think you know it."

"Of course he knows it," Clive groused. "Now, let the poor boy be."

"I'm sorry, Wilford. I didn't mean—"

"Ann, there's nothing to apologize for!" Intentionally, Wilf then changed the subject. "So, you also lived through the war?"

Ann smiled sweetly. "Yes, but as a youngster—Patsy Ann Linley, I was called then. During the war, my mother ran the post office in our village while my father went off to work in a munitions factory. My only sister and I grew up helping her. My only brother, a twin to my sister, had died at birth, so we two girls were all she had.

"At age seventeen I met and married Clive, the good Lord sent us four glorious children—our son Peter and daughters Glenda, Glynis, and Della—and we have been wonderfully happy. Truly, I don't think any couple could be more in love!"

Wilf chuckled. "I don't doubt that for a moment. So, you raised your children here in Cornwall? In Looe, is it?"

"Actually we live in St. Columb, near Newquay," Ann responded, "and have come to Looe on holiday. But Cornwall is not where we reared our children."

Clive laughed heartily. "Not at all. We've only been in Cornwall since I became redundant—no longer needed at my work, you see. Thirty years it's been since I was sacked and lost my salary. So we became self-employed and came here because it is less expensive to live in Cornwall than the rest of England."

"Or *was* less expensive," Ann added with a little sarcasm of her own.

"Quite right. Ann's a chemist, you see. Like myself, Wilford, she grew to maturity up in the Midlands, in Nottinghamshire—"

"Nottinghamshire. Nottingham. Wait a minute! Isn't that Robin Hood country? Where the evil sheriff is supposed to have lived, just outside of Sherwood Forrest?"

"One and the same," Clive chuckled. "Though the sheriff lived in Nottingham Town, while the Forrest lies in the shire or surrounding countryside. We've even taken our children and picnicked a time or two beneath Sherwood's Major Oak, where Robin Hood once camped with his merry men. They say that oak's more than twelve hundred years old, or it was when last we saw it."

"So, are you telling me that Robin Hood was real and not just a legend?" Wilf pressed. Robin Hood, one of his boyhood heroes, was one of the topics he had not read up on since he had decided to visit England. In fact, he hadn't even thought about doing so.

"The legends are usually based upon some sort of reality," Ann stated kindly.

"There are even those who say Robin Hood was aristocratic—Earl of Locksley, you know." Clive was also speaking kindly, patiently. "That adds a great deal of credence to the legends, of course, for only the aristocracy knew how to write and keep genealogies." The man paused, a slight grin on his face. "Of course, those who wrote may have been nothing more than terrible and inveterate liars—authors of fiction, we would no doubt call them today, just as we would call their pathetic lies, best sellers."

"That's quite enough, Clive," Ann said sternly. "Novels and novelists have their place, you know."

"Quite right," Clive winked at Wilf, "though beyond being stuffed under Ann's side of the bed, we won't dare say where that place might be. By the by, we've now passed through two stops without a word, and we shan't have you ignorant of the local geography on our account. The first of the stops was at Causeland and the second at Sandplace, where the river turned tidal."

"Tidal? You mean the sea comes this far inland?"

"Yes," Clive nodded, "when the tide's in, as it is now."

Looking out the window into the gathering twilight, Wilf was stunned to see that the tiny East Looe river had become a water-course perhaps a hundred yards wide. White swans and seagulls were drifting on the water, and near the far bank, a boat of some size was tied to a tree, or at least that was how it looked from the train.

"How deep is it?" he questioned wonderingly.

"Well, that depends on where the river channel runs. In the channel it is much deeper than elsewhere. But on average, I should guess five feet or so, at least as you Americans measure it."

"Five feet, huh. And it's tidal—by the way, one of those strange-looking fellows back in Liskeard called me a Yank. Where did that name come from?"

Clive laughed. " 'Yankee Doodle Dandy' was a popular American song during the war, and it didn't take much for the Brits to shorten it to Yank and apply it to every American they saw. Some still use it, but not many."

"We're slowing down again. Are we at Looe already?"

Ann shook her head. "Not yet. This is just a small crossing—"

But Wilf, still looking out the window, heard no more of Ann's answer. Instead he was staring at the crossing—no, he was staring at a girl who was standing on the road staring back at him.

Blinking, Wilf shook his head, but she did not disappear. Instead, she remained, standing close to the track looking upward, and as the coach stopped for a few seconds, sounded its horn and then started again, their gaze held. For an eternal few seconds it lasted, their eyes locked somehow on each other, and then the train was past and he was craning his neck with his face against the glass, watching until the tracks made a slight curve and she was lost to sight.

Ignoring Ann's startled cry, Wilf lunged to his feet and ran to the end of the coach. Thank the Lord she hadn't moved, he thought, as he watched her trim figure disappear into the gathering dusk. But she hadn't. As a matter of fact, she was still watching him—or at least she was watching the receding train, seemingly intent upon it and nothing else.

With a growing sense of wonder, Wilf watched back, straining his eyes until the darkness and the trees had swallowed her completely. Then he slowly turned and made his way back through the swaying coach, fighting to keep the image of the girl secure in his mind.

"Did you see her?" he started to ask the Paynes, and then he noticed the look of shock and fear on Ann's countenance. "Ann, what is it? What's wrong?"

"Oh, Wilford, dear, you...I...we...we saw her!"

"Who? The girl? Of course we saw her! I...I've got to go back and find her. I think she was trying to tell me something—"

"Wilford," Clive stated quietly, "you won't be finding her. Not, at least, in this world."

"Why not? What do you mean? Who is she?"

Clive shook his head. "Not is, Wilford—was! You see, Cornwall is a haunted land, a country with a past so strange and sometimes bloody no one today could possibly understand."

"What are you trying to tell me?"

"Folks say dusk in Cornwall is the hour of haunts," Ann breathed as she gazed fearfully out the window of the old coach. "It was when as a child I heard our ghost in Nottinghamshire; it is now, when all three of us have seen the tragic ghost of Morwenna Miller!"

Another thing about Wilf Abbott that's important, and then I'm going to stop talking about him so much, is that deep down he's an idealistic dreamer. Trouble is, he's also a pragmatist, and those two qualities make a mighty tough combination. His mind—which shows every indication of brilliance—is always working, pondering, analyzing, studying. I've never known anyone with such a thirst for knowledge. He naturally forms that knowledge into dreams, imagining himself and others as he thinks they should and maybe even could be.

Then the pragmatist in him goes to work, reminding him of the too-human flaws that naturally exist in everyone, himself included. Then he turns pessimistic, and his glorious, idyllic dreams wither away.

On occasion, however—very rarely but sometimes—he follows his dreams, no matter that they make no sense to him or anyone else in this pragmatic world. This, he's told me, was one of those times....

Chapter Three

*I*t was still dark when Wilf opened his eyes, and for a moment he lay without moving, trying to remember where he was. Memory returned then, and he nearly groaned at the thought. Following their combined experience with the girl at the crossing—or ghost, as both Ann and Clive firmly believed—the elderly couple had invited him to stay the night with them, occupying the spare bedroom of a holiday bungalow they had rented. And for some crazy reason—and this was so far from his typical behavior that even Wilf couldn't believe it—he had accepted! From the moment their eyes had met, he hadn't been able to get the girl at the crossing from his mind, and he knew he couldn't continue his journey until he did!

It wasn't that she had been stunningly beautiful, he told himself, though in fact she had been the most incredibly beautiful young woman he had ever seen. Neither had it been the luxurious darkness of her long, flowing hair, or even the liquid blueness of her eyes—eyes which had seemed in the brief moment of their passing to be unnaturally large. Rather, it had been something that had passed between the two of them during those few seconds of time when their gaze had locked upon each other, a strange but incredibly glorious communication.

Pursing his lips, Wilf concentrated, probing his memory to see what else besides the girl's amazingly lovely countenance his mind had captured. She had been standing alone on a paved street that was also a rail crossing, though which crossing it might have been, he had no idea. He knew they had passed both Causeland and Sandplace, for Clive had said so. He also knew that the winding East Looe River had already become tidal at that place. Beyond that, however, all he could remember were a few houses with lighted windows scattered up a wooded hillside behind her and some sort of business sign down near the river. Despite this paucity of information, however, Wilf felt certain he would recognize the place if ever again he saw it.

Only, he wondered in the early morning darkness, would she be there? Or even in the area? Perhaps not, for she had appeared cold to Wilf, too cold to have just come from a warm house or business. After all, she'd had her arms wrapped about herself the way his mother always had after a long wait for his father in the chill of a winter evening, and that could only mean one thing. The girl at the crossing had been out of doors for some time. So, where had she come from, and where in the darkening world of southeast Cornwall had she been going?

And that brought to mind something else. The girl had not only been alone, but she had also looked lonely to Wilf—lonely and perhaps even a little afraid. Yet when their eyes had met through the coach window, even for those brief few seconds, Wilf had sensed a strength or determination that he'd found surprising. There had also been a knowing in those fathomless eyes, a sense of age and harsh experience that one did not often find. Wilf knew, for he carried that look himself, the look of tragedy, his mother had often called it, and during the decade since her and his father's death, Wilf had learned the hard way that those who did not have it, man or woman, could not understand.

And that was the most troubling thing of all, Wilford Abbott thought. Wise and knowing as she had looked, the girl standing alone outside the passing coach had been only a

child—a schoolgirl wearing what he had read was the typical navy blazer over white blouse and grey skirt of all British schoolgirls. So what was he, a world-wise but already weary-of-life American of thirty-four, doing romanticizing about her lovely visage?

"Ohhh," he breathed wearily, "Mother, Mother, Mother. What in heaven's name have you done to me—"

Rolling onto his side, Wilf almost groaned aloud he felt so stiff and sore. Like he'd been run over by a Mac truck, he thought—one of his brother Brig's endless sayings. Of course it was only jet-lag, but being too miserable to remain longer in bed, he arose, stretched his aching muscles, and then dressed.

To the best of Wilf's knowledge, Clive and Ann still slept, so with as little noise as possible he left the bungalow and set out on his own to do a little early-morning exploring. The air was nippy but not cold, and Wilf was pleasantly surprised that it was not raining, something the travel books said happened constantly in Great Britain. Of course, there was a bit of mist over everything, but to a man of the desert the mist seemed pleasant, even enjoyable.

"Granite Henge Holiday Bungalows," he read aloud at the entrance to the group of cottages where Clive and Ann were staying. "Trelawne Cross, Looe, Cornwall. Owners and Operators: David and Jeanette Fellick." Well, he thought, the address might be Looe, but even in the darkness he could tell they were in the country. He could hear cows in the distance, and too many songbirds were already greeting the approaching dawn.

At a nearby crossroads, signs indicated that Looe was one direction, Polperro the other. Since Wilf had seen a bit of Looe and its famous old seven-arch bridge the night before, he swung into the road to Polperro, his long strides quickly eating up the distance. Past another holiday village, he rounded a long curve and dropped down a steep incline to a place called Crumplehorn, which featured an old mill, a hotel, and numerous shops. There was no doubt, he thought with a wry grin, that this was one of the world's myriad tourist attractions, though in former days it must have been a hard-working country village.

Striding through the Crumplehorn roundabout, Wilf turned left toward Polperro and the sea, following a street that was called the Coombes, which Ann had explained meant narrow canyon or ravine. Cars without permits were not allowed where he now moved, and as the street turned into Fore Street, a sign stopped all motor vehicles altogether. And well it should, Wilf thought as he moved along toward the center of town. Never had he seen streets so narrow, so steep. Of course everything about the place was old, built hundreds of years before automobiles had been invented, and Wilf supposed the alleyways—for they could hardly be called anything else—had been fine for carts and horses.

Houses, inns, pubs, restaurants, and an amazing variety of souvenir and other shops lined the way, most of them two to three stories high and, closer to the town center, crowded directly against the narrow streets. For a time, Wilf simply wandered, crossing the River Pol near the Big Green, which boasted Nelson's Restaurant but no grass whatsoever, passing the whitewashed home of someone named Dr. Jonathan Couch, climbing for a way up Landaviddy Lane and Mill Hill before retracing his steps and discovering that toward the harbor the lane became Lansallos Street, with a steeply-climbing alley off to the southward called Little Laney.

Passing an ice cream shop and a pub called Noughts and Crosses, Wilf turned north again, across Roman Bridge, past the House on Props, and then down an extremely narrow street called The Warren, wondering how long it would take for daylight to come, and feeling thankful, as the mists thickened to fog near the harbor, that he had worn his jacket. Even his rapid movements did not seem enough to warm him against the damp humidity of the place. Nevertheless, he couldn't help admiring the ancient whitewashed homes and businesses with their gaudy signs and flags, as well as their gaily-planted window boxes that seemed to reach out across The Warren toward each other. In fact, the layout of old

Polperro appeared so haphazard that Wilf found himself likening the buildings to dozens upon dozens of oddly-sized dice that the Lord had playfully rolled down onto the steep hills during some long-ago game of chance.

Even as he was chuckling over this, however, Wilf was struggling to better understand his motive for being in Polperro in the first place. Yes, he enjoyed traveling and seeing new country. But it was only after passing the narrow harbor, which now that the tide was out was merely a mud flat with boats sitting high and dry, and climbing the incredibly steep lane to the top of Talland Hill, that he was ready to admit the truth.

He was looking for something and was desperate enough that when a girl he had met—the same one he'd mentioned to Clive and Ann—had told him he might find whatever he was looking for in Looe or Polperro, both communities in Cornwall, England, he had become instantly intrigued.

Both, she had told him, were coastal towns on the English Channel. There was only four or five miles of spectacularly rugged coastline between them, and both communities had histories going back many hundreds of years.

So now he was here, which in and of itself was strange enough. But add to it the even more disconcerting encounter he had had with the unknown girl at the crossing, and Wilf was really beginning to wonder. What was going on? Was this all in his head, or had something outside of himself drawn him to this unlikely place?

Of course not! It was *him* that had brought him to Polperro—an aging young man with an ever-increasing need for a deeper understanding of himself—of the inner core that was driving him to be the miserable failure he had become. Until he had that understanding, Wilf was now admitting ruefully, he could not move on—could not begin to make the contribution to life he felt certain he should be making. Or maybe would end up not making, if he didn't get some sort of a move on!

Turning back down the gradually-lightening street, Wilf found himself thinking again of the girl at the crossing, which in and of itself was absolutely insane! He had no earthly hope of ever seeing her again, and even if he did, she was at best a high school student who should have no interest in him at all. Neither, his rational self screamed, should he be interested in her! Not only was it wrong according to every rule of decorum he had ever been taught; it was more than likely illegal, especially here in this land of old laws and rigidly formal traditions.

Yet overriding his inner and very personal quest, the girl's lovely image remained, troubling him, floating always before him, enticing him with quickened heart to find his way back to that nameless crossing—

Below at the wharf—the quay, as Clive had called the same thing in Looe—Wilf could hear the voices of men at work. But resisting an impulse to seek them out and perhaps become a nuisance, he instead started back up The Warren in the direction of Crumplehorn, Trelawne Cross, and the Paynes' bungalow. After all, they might have awakened by now and become worried—

With daylight, the fog seemed to thicken, and Wilf was wondering at that when he had the feeling that he was no longer alone on the narrow street. Glancing behind him, he saw a lighted window set low in a building, advertising pasties, and bending over and gazing into it, her back to him, was a uniformed schoolgirl. Though the mists swirled thickly, Wilf was able to see clearly her dark, cascading hair.

For some reason, the girl straightened up, turned at that instant, and looked directly toward him, and Wilf was thunderstruck. *It was her!* It was the girl from the crossing! Her wide, liquid-blue eyes were the same, her luxuriously dark hair cascading down over her shoulders was the same, even her exquisitely chiseled face and delicate lips, closed but flirting with what might easily become a radiant smile, were exactly as he remembered them from the evening before! But more—and this was what now rooted Wilf to the spot—in the girl's eyes was not only a calm recognition, but from them there was coming again that joyous, peaceful communication that seemed to say, without any words being uttered, *"I am here,*

Wilford Abbott. I have been waiting patiently for a terribly long time, and now you have come home to me at last!"

Drawing a deep breath to still his racing heart, Wilf raised his hand as if to signal, and then he turned and started toward her. Only somehow the mists chose that moment to swirl higher and more thickly; the girl seemed to dim from his view, and scant seconds later when he neared the lighted window, Wilf was stunned to find himself alone.

She was gone! Nowhere on the narrow street was there another human being! Even in the pasty shop he could see no one. Again the mysterious girl had vanished, and Wilf could hardly comprehend what was happening. First at the crossing and now here in Polperro! It was almost as if she were somehow ahead of him, anticipating his arrival in Cornwall and even his early-morning walk! But, that could only mean that she...that she—

With a muttered oath, Wilf fled back through The Warren and onto the steep coastal path, his eyes continuing their search even while his heart drifted into despair. What was happening to him? What sort of crazy, otherworldly game was being played with his mind?

"Mother, Mother, Mother," he breathed as he strode upward, "what are you trying to do? No, the real question is, What *have* you done? What sort of terrible trick did you play on my childishly-believing soul—"

As the coastal path wound and climbed toward a large war monument placed high on the seaside cliffs of Talland Hill, Wilf's boots were soon soaked through, either from dew or the bright mist that was still wafting and thinning before him. Though damp, the mist remained almost pleasant, creating a strange sort of shadowy light that made everything appear mysterious, vague.

Where Wilf climbed, the cliffs and hillside were literally covered with greenery—meadow grass, ivy, sea-thrift, bluebells, bramble bushes and thick, prickly bushes with bright yellow blossoms that were probably the gorse Ann had mentioned the night before—and he found himself wondering how people back in Arizona would react to such natural, luxurious growth. In Arizona almost nothing grew unless it was irrigated, while here on this verdant, almost vertical meadow—

Pausing at the tall stone cross listing those from the area who had given their lives in the two world wars, Wilf breathed deeply, trying to catch his breath. From below he could hear waves from the English Channel crashing into the base of the high cliff on which he stood. Off to his right, Polperro's tiny rock-bound harbor was visible, and the rocky southern coast of Cornwall stretched for miles in both directions, vanishing only where the mists had not yet lifted. Out in the Channel, several ships plied the waters, large tankers and other vessels as well as the smaller fishing boats that had sailed from Polperro, Looe, and other local ports before the tide had gone out.

An island below and to the left carried the name of George's Island or Looe Island, depending on who was asked, while further eastward beyond Looe Bay and its world-famous shark angling club was Whitsand Bay. Beyond that and after a canny little step, as Ann had put it the night before, one came at length to Rame Head and Penlee Point, near where the River Tamar cut County Cornwall off from County Devon.

A quaint legend had it, Clive had told him, that the devil had once come to the Tamar and had stood wondering whether to cross over into Cornwall. "No, I won't risk it," said he. "Over there everyone's made into a saint, everything else into squab pie!"

Turning to the west, Wilf cast his mind in that direction, hoping to break the spell of gloom that seemed to have settled over him. Immediately to the west was a point of land called Pencarrow Head, followed by the fishing village of Fowey. Then came Gribbin Head, St. Austel Bay and town, Black Head, Chapel Point, and way off in the distance to the southwest, Dodman Point. Though it couldn't be seen from there, far beyond Dodman Point lay Falmouth Harbour with its opposing castles, Pendennis and St. Maws, which had been built by Henry VIII to protect the entrance of Carrick Roads—in actuality, a bay or harbor.

Another fair old trot—again Ann's words—beyond Falmouth led one south to the abandoned leper colony at Lizard Point, named not because of reptiles but because of a linguistic corruption of the Old Cornish "Lys ardh," meaning "the high place." A scaly line of cliffs and caves stripped with serpentine paths led to Lizard Point, the most southerly prong of England, and there the Atlantic met the English Channel.

On around to the other side of the small peninsula, one came to St. Michael's Mount, supposedly built by a giant called Cormoran, one of many giants that Cornish folk claimed as real. The huge stones at Lanyon, Mulfra, Madron and Trethevy were said to be their playthings; the giant Trebiggan had arms so long he could pluck sailors from passing ships, and Bolster the giant could stand with one foot on St. Agnes Beacon and the other on Carn Brea. Another giant hid his treasure in Trencrom Castle, Ludgvan, and of course, Clive had laughed, Jack the Giant Killer had been a Cornishman.

Then there was the legend, more recent though hardly more substantiated, that St. Michael's Mount (or Glastonbury in Somerset, depending on whom one asked) was the landing place of a wealthy Jewish trader known to history as Joseph of Arimathea. A friend to the Romans, Joseph, with the assistance of his youthful nephew Jesus, had supposedly established a settlement near St. Michael's Mount (perhaps a place called Carn Euny, Clive wondered?) and another one further north, near modern Preston. There, some claimed, the world's future Savior and Redeemer had lived for a time before returning to Jerusalem to begin his ministry, even marrying and raising a family.

From St. Michael's Mount, one came to the old smuggler's city of Penzance, of Gilbert and Sullivan fame, and finally to the dark granite upthrust at the end of the Cornish Peninsula called simply, for centuries upon centuries, Land's End. It was the very westernmost tip of England, and the next land one could expect to encounter, three thousand miles further west, was Ellis Island and New York City.

From Land's End, of course, the jagged coast of Cornwall curved back around to the north and east, eventually leading past St. Ives and Newquay and tiny Tintagel, and on again all the way up to the Bristol Channel and the border with Wales.

The entire scene, even that which could not possibly be viewed from the lofty headland upon which Wilf stood, would have been breathtaking had he allowed it. Yet he did not, for his mind would not let go of the sweet image of the unknown girl.

Climbing directly upward along a faint trail that departed from the main coastal path, Wilf twisted through huge stands of the yellow-flowered but terribly prickly gorse until the hill finally leveled out and he found himself in a cultivated field. Walking due north across the field, he came to a fence and beyond it a road, which he followed westward past some homes and a rather large building.

Wilf didn't know what made him turn around. But when he did, there behind him in a roadway that intersected his, was the girl. Again she was standing alone, her back turned mostly to him, but this time she was looking down the road as if she were waiting for someone. And though she was a good fifty feet away and he couldn't see her face, Wilf was certain it was her. It had to be! The trim figure was the same, the school uniform looked the same, even her dark cascading hair was exactly as he had seen it only moments before.

Restraining an impulse to shout, Wilf started hurriedly back along the road. His heart was once again pounding, his mouth felt dry, and he could think of absolutely nothing he might say once he got to her. Driven still, he knew he had to get close to her, to gaze into her fathomless eyes, to feel again that incredibly glorious communication—

"Hiya, Belinda!" The shouting voice was male, and Wilf stopped abruptly at the sound of it. "Suss out your maths, did you?"

"Shut yer gob," the girl responded with a laugh. Then, as a blazer-clad young man came from behind a house and approached her, she reached up and plucked the cigarette from his mouth.

"That's my fag!" the boy groused as the girl leaned up and pecked him on the cheek.

"Oiaye," she responded saucily as she pulled back, put the cigarette between her lips, and inhaled deeply. "By the by, you missed a spot with your face-flannel!" Laughing, the girl turned and strode toward the parking lot of what Wilf could now see was a school, her friend tagging closely behind.

Stunned, Wilf remained frozen in his tracks. It was not her! Even from a distance he could see that the face was not the same—not even close. This girl was no more than an immature British teen, the sort of girl he would never on this earth feel an attraction for. Besides, he thought as the girl's exhaled smoke dissipated into the mist, there had been absolutely no feeling when her gaze had passed briefly through his, no soundless communication whatsoever!

"Thank goodness," he found himself thinking.

Shaking his head at the insanity of what had been in his mind, what he had almost done, Wilf turned and strode grimly toward Granite Henge and the bungalow of Clive and Ann Payne. Somehow he had to enlist their help so he could get back to that crossing! Only there, he felt certain, would he find information sufficient to get this nightmare of a girl out of his head.

I've always thought that if a story is worth telling, it ought to contain something about a beautiful woman. Wilf's story does. Now admittedly, beauty is in the eye of the beholder, but more than one man had seen beauty in Kerensa Tansin—rare physical beauty.

On the other hand, though they seem to be growing more scarce, now and then one meets a woman who is wise but innocent—in the world but not of it, as the Good Book says. Though appearances might have indicated otherwise, especially to Wilf Abbott, Kerensa Tansin seemed to have the capacity to be such a woman. Only, she was intent at the moment on an errand of her own, so intent that everything else had been relegated to second place. That included her professional career; it included being twenty-nine and unmarried, and it particularly included her appearance.

In her mind, at least, she had such precious little time....

Chapter Four

*T*hings were not going as she had expected, certainly not as she had grown accustomed to, and Dr. Kerensa Tansin was frustrated. Despite her careful preparations, and despite what she considered the purity of her motives, she was making absolutely no progress. In spite of the fact that she had gone to every pertinent site she was aware of, she had been able to feel nothing, learn nothing! Which meant, she thought wearily, that she would have to begin again! It was almost as if—

In the dappled shade of the Kilminorth Woods, it was cool but warming rapidly under the early morning sun. Strangely, the mists, so typical along the southeast coast of England, had already lifted, and the birds that usually raised such a din had grown silent. The only sounds, were the footfalls and occasional murmurings of the rare passers-by, and even those hushed noises seemed incongruous in the ancient woods.

Yet Dr. Tansin did not pause. Her new assistant, whom she had hired sight unseen when all else had failed, was already a day past due. What she would do if he failed to show, she had no idea. Yet she could not stop—not now! So in spite of the warmth and the stillness, she pressed forward, making her way carefully along the walking path that bordered the tranquil West Looe River.

Ahead of her, the walkway curved sharply, following the meandering course of the small stream. Pausing to adjust both her pack and then her top, which in reality was nothing more than the upper portion of a string bikini, Dr. Tansin took a deep breath and continued. Her destination was the site of an ancient mill and miller's cottage that had once been nestled in the woods a short distance below what was called Tencreek. Of course the mill was gone entirely, washed away in some long-ago flood. And all that remained of the cottage, which according to local tradition had been burned by irate neighbors a century or two before, was a moldering pile of stones and rubble.

Yet if her information was correct, that rubble, Dr. Tansin knew, should be enough—at least for the sort of work she did. The trick was first to find it and then to remain there long enough. Well, she thought ruefully, if all would just go as planned, instead of so disastrously, then she wouldn't need her tardy new assistant at all! Instead she could sack the bloke straight away and smile while she was doing it, for she had not liked the randy tone in his voice when they had spoken on the telephone. Only, he was the only one from Cornwall who had applied and was available on the moment's notice, and she did need someone who was familiar with the area. Why, already she had missed the footpath here in the wood—

Some years before, Dr. Tansin had come to England's Oxford University to do post- doctoral work under the great Dr. Rolland Pinckham, now retired. Before applying, unfortunately, she had not clearly understood the differences between American and British anthropological studies, and that ignorance had caused her a few problems. Whereas American anthropologists studied the lives and social systems of both ancient and modern cultures, frequently working with archaeologists as their counterparts, British anthropologists studied only living cultures, called themselves social anthropologists, and left everything ancient to the archaeologists.

Under Dr. Pinckham's direction, she had accepted this limitation and then forced both her research and her thinking into the new role, providentially selecting the supposed self-consuming hedonism of her own generation as her area of research. In this she had succeeded admirably enough to open even her own mind to the disastrous course society seemed to be taking.

Unable to get the love of ancient cultures out of her system, however, she had at every opportunity visited scores of sites in central and southern England—sites ranging from the Neolithic Stonehenge, Woodhenge, Merry Maidens, and Cerne Giant, a 180-foot long Celtic carving in the chalk hillside near Weymouth, to the more modern Iron Age villages of Chysauster and Carn Euny, near Land's End.

In fact, it had been at Carn Euny, standing in its underground fogou—a circular chamber and underground passage 66 feet long and completely lined with painstakingly-quarried granite—where a fortuitous event had completely altered Dr. Tansin's career. She had been waiting alone for a friend, her hand on one of the granite walls to steady herself, when a sort of heaviness had suddenly overcome her, burdening her with a sense of great and terrible loss. Into her mind, then, had come a clear but very divergent picture of the ancient inhabitants of Carn Euny, devout and peace-loving Christians, she had felt, who were doing what they had done in the fleeting moments before their horrifying deaths at pagan hands some fifteen centuries before.

Saying nothing to anyone, she had decided, on a lark, to write down her impressions, easily tying them in with the on-site research so tediously recorded by the archaeologists. Dr. Pinckham had discovered her paper, liked it, and without her permission had submitted it for publication in a prestigious scientific journal. It had been accepted and, suddenly as that, Dr. Tansin had found herself awash with fame.

Nearly three years had now passed; other similar "impressions" had come at other sites, and were particularly vivid when she had gone out of her way to play the part of those she was studying. These also had been published and, because of them, Dr. Tansin had been honored with memberships in two extremely distinguished international societies—the

National Academy of Sciences and the Society of Social Anthropologists—and she had post-doctoral students clamoring to come to Oxford to study under her.

Now, though, a new problem had entered Dr. Tansin's life, one that was proving to be a great perplexity. For weeks on end, something within her had been saying that she was through in England—that it was time for her to move on, both professionally and personally. Only she had no idea just where she wanted to go. There were too many qualifiers and quantifiers, too many unknown factors, to make the decision easy.

Besides, there was this one last project that needed sussing out, especially if she were to end up leaving the area. Already she had put it off so many times it was embarrassing, though she had no real idea what made her feel that way. But if she were truly going to be leaving—

"Pardon me," she asked an elderly couple who were approaching her along the walkway, smiling sweetly as she spoke, "I seem to have lost my way. Could you perhaps direct me to the remains of the Miller's Cottage? I have been told it is near here, but I cannot seem to suss out the path."

Doing her best to ignore their hushed but scornful comments about her scanty attire, Dr. Tansin followed the elderly couple back down the worn walkway to where she was directed onto an almost nonexistent path—one she had definitely missed. Thanking the couple, she did not hurry but started carefully along the obscure pathway toward the river, her every sense alert for whatever might occur.

Above her, the thick trees admitted only the most filtered light, the lush undergrowth effectively muted the sound of her passing, and in the trees the birds continued their unusual silence, apparently too burdened by something or other, to complain. The whole situation seemed eerily somber, even haunted. Yet none of it surprised or even phased Dr. Tansin. In places of much more ancient traumas and misdeeds, as well as the habitations of those who had perpetrated or suffered through them, there seemed always to be a heaviness in the air, a sense of foreboding that she could actually feel. It was almost as though the dead were still being troubled by those ancient events, as though they were anxious to make their sorrows known.

Why would it be any different with the dead of this project, she reasoned as she glided along the almost invisible trail. What difference did it make if the inhabitants had been gone two thousand years, two hundred, or even merely two? If they had died miserably, or if other problems had unsettled their lives at the time of their deaths, then it seemed to her that their spirits—their ghosts as most called them—would quite naturally continue a restless wandering that would end only with—with what? Dr. Tansin wasn't exactly certain of the answer, except that she felt her writings, somehow, had given a great many of them a certain measure of peace.

Hopefully, she thought as she paused with one foot on a flat stone that had no doubt been a doorsill before the cottage beyond it had been burned and then tumbled into rubble, her current work would also bring peace. Not only for herself, for she had indeed felt troubled since hearing of this situation, but for the restless spirits of all those who were in some way connected with this lovely place!

Chapter Five

"Ann's where?" Wilf had just arrived back at the holiday bungalow, and had been surprised to find Clive alone. "I thought you said last evening she was a chemist."

Clive chuckled. "And so I did. On this side of the pond, a chemist means a druggist, or one who runs what we used to call an apothecary—a drug store. Ann comes to Polperro each summer to give the local chemist a holiday break—and so I get a holiday as well."

"You don't help her out?"

"Me?" Clive feigned mortified shock. "Of course I help! Most mornings I drive her down in my trusty Passat, and most evenings I retrieve her and tuck her safely into bed. But I don't run the drug store, not at all. Ann's the one who runs it, just as she runs me and most everyone else."

"I'll bet," Wilf smiled. For a moment he hesitated, feeling a natural reluctance to reveal even a little of his private thoughts. Only, this elderly man was proving himself a true friend; besides, Wilf had no idea where else to turn. His experiences with the unknown girl were already more troubling than he could believe.

"Clive, I…uh…I saw her again."

"Excuse me, dear boy? It's the hearing, you know. First thing to go after the memory. Now, what was that I just said? Or was it you?"

Wilf smiled ruefully. "The girl at the crossing, Clive. I saw her again, down in Polperro."

"Are you certain?" the elderly hero asked, instantly perplexed.

"Absolutely. It was early this morning, and she was standing in front of a pasty shop either on Fore Street or The Warren, I can't remember."

Clive nodded. "I know the place well. Built down in the ground like a half-cellar, so from the street you gaze down into it. Wonderful pasties, though I wouldn't touch one for the world! Bad for the figure, you know. Did you speak with her?"

Soberly Wilf shook his head. "I tried, but as I started toward her the mists swirled up, and the next thing I knew, she was gone. And I mean gone! I could find no sign of her anywhere!"

"Isn't it lovely?" Clive grinned mischievously.

"What?" Wilf groused. "Are you back to that crazy ghost thing?"

"Aren't you?"

Vehemently Wilf shook his head. "Absolutely not!"

"Hmm. Well, then, how would you go about describing a mysterious, beautiful schoolgirl who seems able to appear and disappear at will?"

"I didn't say she was beautiful!"

"You didn't need to." Clive smiled wisely. "Remember, Wilford, I saw her, too. Of a truth, I must conclude with my Ann that you've run dead on into one of our lively and more attractive British ghosts."

"You actually believe in such things?" Wilf asked uncomfortably.

"Hello. Of course I do. Remember, my Patsy Ann grew up with a ghost. You see, their home in the village in Nottinghamshire, the one with the post office, was five hundred years old when Ann's father purchased it. Centuries earlier it had been an inn—a stopping place for weary travelers who were dropped there by their equally weary coachmen."

Clive beamed his enthusiasm. "Why, you should just see the place—stuccoed and timbered on the outside and heavy oak beams hanging low from the ceilings inside. Each beam is black with five centuries of smoke and grime. The mews or stables out back are gone, but the inn remains strong, three stories high with the attic, and every room quaint and mysterious."

"And the ghost?"

"Thank goodness he isn't a mean one," Clive declared soberly. "Some are, you know. But this one? He doesn't do much more than traipse up and down the halls, banging back and forth and now and again ringing the broken doorbell, just to stir folks up. Folks say he's a coachman who died in one of the rooms and can't find his way out. Myself, though, I think he's in fact a woman—a chamber maid, I dare say—who is still banging her broom around, trying to get the place cleaned up before the master returns."

"Anybody ever see her? Or him, as the case may be?"

"Not that I've heard, at least no one other than my Patsy Ann. She claims to have caught a glimpse of something one day, though I can't say if she's serious or only nattering on a bit."

"Well, there's the difference." Wilf was serious. "We've seen this girl with our own eyes, Clive. All three of us! And now I've seen her a second time! She's no ghost, and I know it!"

"Except that without much effort she gets around to wherever you just happen to be," Clive added softly. "Then, too, she can appear or disappear at will. Finally, rumors are flying willy-nilly that others have seen this lovely apparition in recent months, though I won't be accountable for their fanciful tales."

For a moment the room was filled with an uncomfortable silence. Wilf, who was actually beginning to entertain the same impossible thoughts, did not know what to say. Desperately, therefore, he changed the subject.

"Clive," he ventured carefully, "would you mind if I asked you a personal question?"

"So long as it's not so personal that I must reveal my mortal sins and shortcomings," Clive responded with a wink. "Such doings are between me and the Good Lord, and even he doesn't know the half of them."

Smiling at Clive's almost continuous droll humor, Wilf nodded. "If you think it's as personal as that, then I won't expect an answer."

"Fair enough."

"Last evening on the train," Wilf began, "you and Ann spoke of what had passed between you when you first met. I would like very much to know more about that event."

"Hello? How we met, you mean?"

"No...well, yes, if you'd like to tell me that. But what I'm really after is a better understanding of the communication that each of you experienced, the feeling that led you to know you were meant for each other."

Now Clive smiled. "Lovely, lovely. I thought I detected a rather keen interest from you when Ann brought it up. You've had such a communication, then? Perhaps with our fair ghost?"

"I...uh...I didn't say that."

"Not with so many words, perhaps." Clive smiled warmly. "Be that as it may, you're the one who asked the question, and I'll not answer it with another, the way you Americans do. First, Wilford, what myself and Ann experienced is a rare thing, not given to many. Why it came to us, I don't know. It just did, and for more than fifty years I've been glad of it!

"Secondly, what Ann experienced was not precisely the same as what I did—or at least I've never thought so. However, it may be that we simply use different words to describe it. I don't know, for I've no way of getting into her head, or thank the good Lord, of her getting into mine."

Wilf chuckled. "That could be a bit unnerving."

"Quite right. Or devastating, especially if I were to learn that Ann didn't feel toward me as she's always claimed." For a moment or so Clive was silent, his gaze lingering on but not seeing something across the room.

"As far as my own perceptions of that moment when we met, I believe I need to explain a few things before I can describe them. As she told you last evening, I was older, nearly twenty-nine when I first laid eyes on my Patsy Ann. I'd been around the world a bit, fought in a cruel war on two continents, and seen terrible, terrible things. I'd also seen a great many beautiful women who had absolutely nothing I felt I wanted, and though I'd squired a few of the better element from time to time, none had much appeal for me. My supposition is that you have encountered the same."

Soberly Wilf nodded his acknowledgment.

"Perhaps it was those long years of loneliness that contributed to the power of what I felt," Clive continued. "Certainly that would make sense. But no matter. When I first clapped eyes on my Patsy Ann, I saw not a pretty child of seventeen or even a youthful woman of unsurpassed beauty. What I saw, Wilford, was home!"

"Home?" Wilf was thunderstruck, but tried not to show it. The thing was, he'd had that same sort of feeling as the train had carried him past the girl at the crossing.

"Right!" Clive chuckled. "Now, don't think me daft, for I'm doing my best to describe a thing that I've always believed is best left to the sensitivities of women. Nevertheless, when I first saw my Ann, I most definitely saw her physical beauty and was attracted to it. That had happened before, however, for there are a great many young and beautiful women in this world, and it is not what moved me. What did, was the sense that with this delightfully lovely young woman, I had come home at last—not just home from the wars in Africa and Northern Europe, but home from the wars of life. There was assurance in her eyes, as she gazed at me, that spoke to my very soul—of peace, happiness, security, contentment, and yes, even of love!"

"So, it was a romantic sort of feeling?"

Clive was silent, thinking. "Not really," he finally responded. "At least, not at first. Certainly romance entered in very quickly, and a deep sense of it remains with us even today. In that first few seconds, however, the feeling was more of a welcoming home, a wondrously joyful reunion of two souls that I still feel had been meant for eternity to come together. It was as though I already knew Ann's heart, and she, mine. And of a truth, Wilford, in all the years since that day, I don't believe either of us has ever actually surprised the other."

"Interesting," Wilf acknowledged quietly. "I once heard my mother claim the same thing—that she'd never been surprised by what was hidden in Dad's heart."

"I daresay. The only other emotion I recall, was the feeling that I wanted to protect her. Somehow my Patsy Ann gave me purpose—not a career sort of thing, mind you—but more a sense that I wanted to do for her everything I ever could and give her everything I would ever have. As I consider it now, I suppose it was about responsibility. Somehow I knew that I wanted to be responsible for her in every way possible for the rest of our lives, and the thought absolutely thrilled me!"

"So, there was a sense of joy in what passed between you?"

"Joy?" Again the elderly man chuckled. "Wilford, until that moment I'd never felt real joy! It was a glorious experience, filled with hope and promise such as I'd never imagined might exist! More, what I've taken several moments to describe for you—to dissect and pull apart, as it were—passed between Ann and me in scant seconds! And whereas my meager attempt at description has been woefully inadequate, what actually happened, at least for me, was so much more that I will never in this life find words for the describing of it."

In amazement, Wilf pondered Clive's words. If he could have somehow opened up the top of his head, exposed his two experiences with the unknown girl, and then asked this elderly man to describe what was showing, Wilf was certain the words would have remained as Clive had spoken them. Somehow, more than a half century as well as continents, oceans and cultures apart, Clive and Ann Payne, and now he and the unknown girl, had experienced a remarkable something that was tangentially the same!

"Very well," he finally continued, his fingers drumming the table as he pondered, "here's another question. Do you believe that Ann was the only one for you? That you were meant for each other and no one else?"

Clive smiled. "I didn't say that. True, it's a question I've asked myself a hundred times and more. And the only answer I can give with honesty is, I don't know. My belief, however, is that Ann was the only one for me *at that precise time!* Should she have been uninterested, or should some other unfortuitous event have driven us apart, I'm quite certain that each of us would have found another."

"And experienced the same degree of joy?"

"I would hope so. Of course our experiences would have been different. But in the justice of God, if each of us were doing our best to honor our commitment to our spouses, as Ann and I have done these fifty-three years, remaining faithful in all things, then certainly we should have experienced similar joy."

"Then," and Wilf was watching Clive's eyes as he asked this, "you believe that joy comes from marital fidelity?"

Clive smiled tenderly. "Ahh, Wilford, I don't believe that is a question I wish to pursue."

"Why not?"

"Because when I pursue it with my own children, some of them accuse me of preaching. I am afraid they may be right."

"Well," Wilf chuckled, "I don't suppose there's anything wrong with a good preachment now and then. Besides, as my brother Brig likes to put it, I've paid for the ticket, so I might as well go for the ride."

"And we say, 'In for a ha'penny, in for a pound.'" Soberly Clive regarded Wilf. "Still, it's a topic I don't believe I'm prepared to visit. My Ann, though—well, she'd wax eloquent about it any time you asked."

Chapter Six

"Wax eloquent about what?"

Instantly Clive was on his feet. "Ahh, my dear Ann, I was just telling young Wilford that you were busily engaged in the excruciating day-long work of a chemist. Now here you come to make me the liar."

"You don't need any help with that," Ann replied sweetly. "Would you care for a spot of tea, Wilford?"

"No, thank you."

"Hot chocolate, then? That's what Clive and I drink, you know."

Wilf smiled. "If you're going to be having some, then I'd be happy to join you."

Ann smiled and was soon bustling about the small kitchen, preparing hot water and three dainty cups of china. "Wilford, dear, I know you named your family last evening," she queried as she scurried about, "but this morning I can't seem to recall them—none, that is, but your sister Annie."

"You would remember her," Clive teased. "But before Wilford tells us more, my dear, how is it that you're here in our lovely bungalow before the end of the day?"

"Today was for once again familiarizing myself with the accounts," Ann repied with her customary sweetness.

"Tomorrow the work begins, so I had a taxi bring me home. Now, Wilford, if my husband's almost insatiable curiosity has been properly satisfied—"

"Yes, Wilford," Clive grinned, "do tell us more!"

"Very well." Wilf could not believe he was doing this. Yet in the worst way he needed their help. "As I told you on the train, my folks are dead—killed in an auto accident several years ago."

"That must have been very difficult for you children."

"Yeah," Wilf acknowledged, "it was tough. But except for the two youngest, we were mostly grown. Since then Hebe, Brig, and Annie and their spouses have finished raising Julie and Zo, while I've watched over myself."

"And done a lovely job of it, too!"

Wilf grinned at Clive's spontaneous and almost constant sarcasm. "Thank you, Clive, though there are those who would differ with you."

"Well, what are the rantings of millions when compared with the perceptive opinion of myself, I always say."

"Zo?" Ann then asked, ignoring her husband altogether.

"Lorenzo."

"Oh, you Americans," she exclaimed, "always shortening good, honest names. We English folk would rarely think of doing such a thing."

Wilf smiled. "You would if you'd been given ours. I don't know where the folks came up with them, but Annie's is the only name we ever made longer. We still call Melissa, Missy.

"She is the child who died?"

Soberly Wilf nodded. "I don't suppose it would have been easy for my folks to lose any of us. But losing Missy, her being the baby—well, Mom never got over it, and I don't suppose Dad did, either. He just didn't talk about it as much."

"And you?" Clive asked quietly.

"Well, yeah," Wilf squirmed, "I miss her, at least when I think about her. Mostly I try not to—"

"Okay, let me see if I have all of you right," Ann stated quickly as she forced a smile. "Ann is the eldest, followed by

Heber, Brigham, you, Lorenzo, Julie, and of course sweet little angel Melissa."

Wilf smiled. "Good for you, Ann. I have a cousin who has never remembered us that well."

Ann giggled. "Yes, I'm sure. Now, what is this Clive has been telling you I'd wax eloquent over?"

"Oh," Wilf responded, feeling reluctant to even bring it up again, "it was just a question I asked—nothing very important."

"Of course it was important," Clive declared emphatically. "Wilford and I have been nattering on about how you and I felt when we met each other. One thing led to another, we got to speaking of the true joy of our union, and then he brazenly asked me a question I thought impertinent!"

"And it was?" Ann pressed as she poured the heated water over the spoonful of chocolate in each of the three cups.

"If we believe that such true joy comes only from marital fidelity."

"Why, of course we do!" Ann seemed startled that her husband had not been willing to respond to the question. "Our answer, Wilford, is a resounding yes! We are most certain that marital fidelity brings joy in every possible way!"

"Why?" Wilf was surprised at the woman's vehemence.

Ann smiled. "Peace, serenity, trust, security, happiness— these wonderful emotions are what comprise true joy, Wilford, and they cannot exist in a heart that is not absolutely faithful."

"Wait a minute," Wilf said as he held up his hand. "You say that joy is comprised of peace, trust—"

"Peace, trust, serenity, security, and happiness. If an individual is not experiencing these sweet emotions, then I don't see how it is possible for him to be experiencing joy."

"And of course, the opposite is also true," Clive added, for some reason no longer reluctant to speak. "When such emotions are lacking, then joy is out the window and the individual feels only misery!"

"Yes," Wilf breathed thoughtfully as he considered his own past fourteen years, "that would make sense."

"But remember, Wilford," Clive went on after he had taken a sip of chocolate, "this marital faithfulness is more than a sexual commitment—much more! It involves charity, or pure and unselfish love and respect for those outside of oneself, beginning first and foremost with one's mate and then extending to all others. It involves integrity, or the willingness to wholeheartedly embrace, think, and even speak truth, despite the inconvenience of it."

"It also requires complete fidelity,"Ann added quietly, "which means that one must remain true to one's companion in both heart and mind, despite the vicissitudes or seeming unfairness of life."

"Quite right!" Clive agreed. "I know a man who left his wife after multiple sclerosis had decimated her body, excusing himself by declaring that she was no longer 'fun.' Even if he had never had another sexual union, that man was filled with infidelity—or more pointedly, he had proven himself an infidel! Quite literally, he had placed himself beyond the pale of joy."

"Do you understand what Clive is saying, Wilford?"

"I'm afraid he's talking too straight not to."

"Then here's a little more straight talk," Clive went on. "In advance, I apologize to my Patsy Ann for being so blunt, for I know she'd rather not discuss this particular issue. Still, in for a ha'penny, in for a pound."

"And I did buy the ticket," Wilf grinned.

"Brilliant. As a final thought, for an individual to be faithful there *must* exist chastity or virtue, which I have learned is best defined as sexual modesty, decency, and propriety. Such sexual behavior, especially when it culminates in a sexual union between a man and woman, is at the same time physical, emotional and even spiritual. It is so eternally powerful and life-giving, both for the couple and for the children they may produce, that to engage in any part of it outside the bonds of matrimony is to desecrate and make a mockery of everything that is sacred and holy!"

"Again, Clive, there are a lot of people in this world who would disagree with you," Wilf declared softly.

"Yes," Ann agreed, "and that exact same number of foolish souls believe that a fleeting moment's pleasure, or even a vast number of them, equate to a lifetime and more of the exquisite joy Clive and I have been endeavoring to describe. It does not so equate, Wilford! Such miserable people waste and wear out their lives running from one intimate encounter to another, vainly seeking through heinous behaviors that have been misnamed alternate lifestyles, the very rewards that come so naturally to those who choose to remain maritally faithful."

Clive smiled sadly. "What such sorry folk cannot know or understand, Wilford, is the beautifully liberating peace that comes from being true and chaste—to oneself as well as to one's mate. They cannot grasp the notion that serenity, trust, security, happiness, and peace are the fruits of marital fidelity, and will grow on no other tree!"

Quizzically Wilf regarded his hosts. "Your implication is that this also applies to those who are unmarried."

"Such as yourself?" Clive chuckled. "Obviously, it must. If one is to honor and be perfectly true to one's chosen mate, can it make any difference if that mate has died, or has not yet been found?"

Stunned, Wilf regarded the man. He could not count the number of times he had been mocked for his own virginity or listened to the concept of virginity being mocked generally. Yet never—not one time—had he been able to think of a defense that was as comprehensive yet simple as the one he had just heard. A person remained chaste because that was the best and most appropriate way to honor one's mate—whether past, present or future, it did not matter!

"And if someone has made a mistake?" Wilf then asked, thinking of his brother's ex- wife but knowing that if it had not been for his mother and her determined stance, he might just as easily be thinking of himself.

"Then one changes as rapidly and as thoroughly as one can," Ann responded fervently, "abandoning his self-serving behavior and wholeheartedly re-embracing integrity, charity, fidelity and chastity—the core values of a happy life. In short, Wilford, one begins again to stand for what is right—and for doing it despite the contrary clamoring of the world. The joy or happiness we have been speaking of can come in no other way!"

"How do you know these things?" Wilf breathed. "How do you know they are true?"

"Because for more than fifty years we've been either living or observing both sides of them," Clive replied quietly as he pushed his empty cup and saucer away and rose to his feet. "Believe me, Wilford; we know!

"Now, something tells me you'd like to revisit that crossing on the East Looe." Clive's eyes twinkled merrily. "If Ann's not too busy, and if you promise not to drag those massive cowboy boots through any holes you may find in the floorboards, I do believe the old Passat might be up to the journey."

Chapter Seven

"Very well, Wilford, I would say that this is the place."

For a moment or so Wilf sat silently, eyeing the railroad crossing from the grassy verge where Clive had stopped his car. It had been interesting driving into Looe in the daylight, for nothing appeared as he remembered it from the night before. The road from Trelawne Cross had wound steeply down a tree-covered bluff to the harbor, which was much larger than the one in Polperro, and then had crossed eastward over the seven-arched stone bridge he recalled from the night before. To the right before the bridge, rows of shops and businesses stretched along the quay, while after the bridge, more shops, restaurants, pubs and businesses ran along another Fore Street as well as up the steep Barbican hill to the east, their lines unbroken along the quay clear to where the harbor opened into Looe Bay and the English Channel. To the left of the bridge, the road—in that direction called Station Road—passed other shops and pubs, as well as the train station, before leaving Looe and winding upward past St. Martin and on to the small crossing where they were stopped.

Like in Polperro, with the tide still out, boats were simply left sitting in the mud. Of course the tide was now starting back in, but the wide mud flats were still much in evidence, as they were in this innocuous-looking place where the single coach of the Looe Valley Line crossed a narrow country lane—the crossing where, the evening before, all of them had seen the unknown girl.

"Goodness," Ann stated from the rear seat of the Passat, "it certainly doesn't look very mysterious in the daylight."

"No," Wilf agreed somberly, "it does not."

"Hardly a likely place for one of our famous Cornish ghosts to put in her appearance, I should say!"

Wilf chuckled without much humor. "Further evidence that she isn't a ghost. If you don't mind, Clive, I'd like to look around a little."

"Very well. Ann has some errands to accomplish in Looe. We can return for you when she is finished—"

Shaking his head, Wilf opened the car door. "There's no need for that, thank you. I can easily walk back to Looe and then to the bungalow, for it isn't all that far. On the other hand, a few moments ago we passed a pub where a bus was stopped—"

"Coach, my dear Wilford. Here such conveyances are called coaches."

Wilf grinned. "Very well—coach. Anyway, you folks run along and have fun, and one way or another I'll see you later this evening."

The crossing, once Wilf was alone to study it, seemed hardly worth noting. In fact, if Clive hadn't known with certainty that this was it, Wilf would have been sure it was further up the East Looe River and would have continued on by.

The road going off the T-shaped intersection that led west over the tracks was small, a narrow lane that arched over a small bridge under which ran the diminutive East Looe River, and then continued across the wide mud flats to the tree-shrouded bluff on the far side. There several small boats lined the shore—boats that Wilf could now see were old and rotted, one having sat so long without use that it had bent like cardboard to fit the hump of the mud bank on which it rested.

The road itself, Wilf noticed as gulls and other shore birds circled overhead, was hardly wide enough for vehicles to pass in opposite directions. Of course British cars, coaches, and lorries were considerably smaller and more narrow than the American vehicles he was used to and so could pass more easily. Besides, he thought as he moved toward the rail crossing, there seemed hardly enough traffic on this road to create a problem.

At the tracks, he was again amused that the train had to stop as well as the automobiles, but the stop signs were there for the conductor as well as the motorists to follow, and he could clearly recall the train stopping and sounding its horn or whistle just as he had noticed the unknown girl.

For some time, Wilf stood without moving, getting his bearings and doing his best to see whatever the young woman might have been seeing besides the passage of his train. And of a truth, there wasn't much to see. Westward from the crossing, the narrow road passed a weathered sign indicating "Trenant Park—Traditional Country Cottages." From there it wound upward over the tree-shrouded bluff and on to Duloe, passing several homes or holiday cottages on its way—Wilf couldn't yet tell which.

Eastward the road ended at the intersection, the bluff on the east of the river looming above it. The larger road Clive had been following then ran north to Liskeard or else eastward, passing either through or by the villages of Morval and Widegates before ending up in Torpoint and Plymouth in Devon County. Or at least that was what the map Clive had given him indicated. Going south, the road passed the pub where he had seen the coach—*The Copley Arms*, the sign in front of it said—then a turnoff to the east to a place called St. Martin, and on beyond that was Looe and the coast.

The girl at the crossing, as Wilf was now calling her, had been facing westward toward the river, and so her lovely face had been toward what little had remained of daylight. Which was good, Wilf thought as he crossed the river and started slowly up the bluff to the west, which seemed as good a place to start as any. At least he had been able to see her beauty—her finely chisled features, as well as her amazingly incredible eyes!

On the other hand, his mind groaned, maybe it would have been a thousand times better if he hadn't seen her at all! Then he wouldn't be undertaking this idiotic search, wasting the precious time he had allotted for seeing Cornwall and the rest of Great Britain.

The homes on the bluff west of the crossing, as he came to them, turned out for the most part to be holiday cottages or bungalows. Nevertheless, it would be at the doors of each of them, he was now admitting with some trepidation, where he would most likely be forced to begin his search.

Unless, he thought without any hope at all, he might just happen to run into her.

Though Wilf would deny this vehemently, it should be obvious by now how unfailingly tender and courteous he is with women—for instance, Ann Payne. Doesn't seem to matter what they look like, what color or how old they are, or even how they might be acting at the moment. It's almost like he reverences them—or at least he reverences those who honor themselves. The others, and in his opinion these have become practically universal, he still treats with courtesy until they have thoroughly disproven themselves, after which he goes out of his way to avoid them!

Thing is, that process can take quite a long time–

Chapter Eight

"Well, if it ain't Joe Bloggs, just when I thought I was shut of you for good. You look whacked as an old wellie, mate, but I'm glad you came to play with the point of me new blade!"

Wilf almost groaned at the sight of the orange-haired youth who had grabbed Ann's handbag the afternoon before. But as an obviously new switchblade appeared in his hand and he dropped into his familiar crouch, Wilf became wary.

"I thought you were in jail where you belonged," he groused as he watched the youth inching closer, meanwhile exhibiting all the telltale signs of an impending lunge. They were outside *The Copley Arms*, where Wilf had hoped to obtain at least a coach ticket, if not some information about the unknown girl. For two fruitless hours he had traipsed about the bluffs west of the river knocking on doors, he was sticky and tired, and thus far he'd learned absolutely nothing! And now to encounter this young idiot again? Was there no justice in life? Not ever?

"There wasn't enough evidence," the sallow young man sneered, "so the coppers let us go."

"Not enough evidence?" Wilf growled, justifiably upset. "What did they want—my boots with your filthy skin on their soles?"

"No," Petroc sneered, "but maybe if I have a bit of your blood on my blade, mate, I can charge you with assault!"

"Yeah, right."

"Too bad my brother didn't cut your heart out yesterday," Petroc continued to grumble. "The nit! Now I have to do the job, and get it done before my honest work begins."

"If nit means stupid, friend, your brother's got no edge on you. And I'll give odds you haven't done an honest day's work in all your miserable life!"

"What? Why, you filthy, stinking—"

"The knife!" Wilf interrupted, stepping forward and pointing at the youth's switchblade with his fingers. "If it's so new, how come it's already broken?"

As Orange-hair automatically dropped his gaze to his knife, Wilf took another quick step and thrust viciously with his already-outstretched fingers, slamming the unwary youth hard in the throat. His eyes opening wide with shock and pain, the young man dropped his knife, uttered a short, strangled cry, and grabbed for his throat, which in the next instant was admitting no air to his suddenly-starved lungs. He tried to cry out but couldn't, his face turned bright and then dark red, and he collapsed like a wet rag when Wilf shoved him toward the ground.

"Here," Wilf grumbled as he knelt and none-too-gently pushed the youth's chin up and back, stretching his throat and re-opening his airway. "Next time you pull a knife on me, you slimy punk, I won't be so charitable! Now roll over, because in a minute you'll be vomiting, and I'll be dogged if I'm going to help you breathe through that filth!"

Rising, Wilf toed Orange-hair over onto his side, and seconds later the much-pierced youth was retching violently into the tall grass, his entire body convulsing with the effort. Good! Wilf was thinking. Maybe next time—

"Impressive," a feminine voice declared from behind him, "but I hope he isn't dead. Assistants are getting harder and harder to come by."

Turning in surprise, Wilf saw a scantily-clad woman—or girl, he wasn't sure which—coming out of the door of the pub.

"Good afternoon, Montana," she said as she moved slowly forward. Man-like, she then thrust out her hand. "I'm called Ren, and this poor boy on the ground that you have practically killed, is Petroc Penryn; Petroc for short. I assume you have a good reason for all this violent mayhem?"

Taken back, Wilf could do little more than stare at the appearance of this second modern hippie. The girl—for now she seemed about the same age as her orange-haired friend—appeared every bit as dirty and unkempt. Thin but not gaunt, she looked to be about five feet two or three inches tall and was dressed in short shorts and a scanty bikini top that, if not bizarre, was most certainly not what he considered modest. Worn sandals graced her dirty feet, a baseball cap covered her hair, her ears sported a single pair of the strangest dangly earrings he had ever seen, and the picture was completed with the addition of very dark sunglasses, the wrap-around variety, which Wilf was to learn she seemed to wear constantly.

"Arizona," he finally mumbled as he took her proffered hand, hoping it was not as dirty as the rest of her appeared. "I'm from Arizona, not Montana."

"Then Arizona it is," she replied as she gave Wilf a grip that surprised him.

"As far as Orange-hair is concerned," Wilf then explained, "he came after me with a knife."

"A knife?"

"Yeah," Wilf growled as he bent and picked up the shiny new weapon, "this switchblade! Naturally, ma'am, I disarmed him—that, and maybe taught him a little something about who not to try his funny-business with in the future."

"I would hope he's learned! Was he trying to rob you, then?"

"Naw, just kill me, is all."

"But, I don't understand—"

Wilf grinned. "You sure don't, not if you've hired him as your assistant. Orange-hair and I first met yesterday afternoon when he and his equally ugly younger brother grabbed a purse from an elderly lady at the train station in Liskeard. Naturally I stopped him and took back the woman's purse—"

By now the woman's mouth was gaping in surprise, and Wilf could hardly keep a smile from his face. "The bruise and scabs on his wrist were caused by my boot, ma'am, when I pinned him to the concrete platform so I could free the purse. His nose is all taped up because the edge of my ring tore out a couple of his nose decorations when I slapped him one. Then when I let him up he came after me with his knife, so this little episode today is the second chapter in what I hope will be a very short story. If there's ever a third, friend Orange-hair will stay down a whole lot longer than this, I promise!"

"And to think I entrusted him," the girl breathed. Then, brightening, she looked back at Wilf. "Are you in Cornwall on holiday, then?"

"Uh, yeah, sort of. Ren. Is that a common name here in England?"

"Common enough, at least here in Cornwall. It's short for Kerensa—Kerensa Tansin."

"Kerensa Tansin." Wilf eyed the girl, doing his best to keep his eyes off her too-obvious figure. "It...uh...has a nice sound."

"Thank you. So does Arizona. A bit twangy, perhaps, but nice."

To soften her barb, the girl smiled, and Wilf was relieved to see that unlike Orange-hair, at least her teeth were clean. They were also white and very even, and he found himself thinking that some poor father had paid out a bundle on orthodontics before losing the rest of his spoiled daughter to the waste-land of punk rockers and hippiedom.

"My name's Wilford," he continued to keep himself from chuckling at the thought. "Wilf Abbott. You're from around here, then?"

"In a manner of speaking." Abruptly Kerensa changed the subject. "I left bangers and mash in the pub for Petroc, but since he doesn't look up to taking nourishment right now, Wilford Abbott, you're welcome to them."

"Thank you, but no," Wilf responded instantly, too dumbfounded by the strange offer to know what else to say.

"Well, cheerio, then." The girl called Kerensa turned and moved nonchalantly off, leaving Wilf with the vague sense of something left undone. It was—

"Hey, wait a minute!" he called after her. "What are you going to do about this—about your assistant?"

"Are you daft?" She questioned as she turned to face Wilf again. "You've already done it. All that needs doing now, is to give him a hundred quid for showing up, and then to send him packing."

"He really is your assistant?"

"Well, he contacted my office two weeks ago in response to my advert, and he had the good graces to show this afternoon, even if it was a day and a half late. Therefore, the answer is yes."

"But...why would you need an assistant?"

"Though no concern of yours," Kerensa Tansin replied, her tone abruptly cooler, "I'm a doctor from the university. Oxford. I took Petroc on to help me with my work."

"You...you're a doctor?"

"What is it? Don't I look doctorly enough for you?"

"No...I mean, what sort of doctor?"

"I have a Ph.D. in anthropology," she replied icily, "and when not in Cornwall I am doing post-doctoral work in social anthropology at Oxford. Now, if you've changed your mind about the bangers and mash—"

"Bangers and mash? I don't even know what that means!"

"Sausage and mashed potatoes."

"Oh. I...uh...you aren't eating?"

"I've already eaten, thank you!"

Wilf nodded his head. "Me, too. You...uh...you don't look much like a professor."

"You already implied that!" The girl cocked her head to the side, her face turned up toward him, and Wilf found himself wishing the dark lenses were gone so he could get some idea of what she was thinking. The unusual glasses, however, were far too dark for him to glimpse anything through. Despite her obviously lush figure, he wasn't interested in her as a woman, of course, but he couldn't help feeling a continued curiosity.

"Would you care to explain yourself?"

"Oh, I don't know," he responded lamely. "The clothes, I guess, and your age."

"As if either of those things mattered at all!"

"Not to some people, I suppose."

"But age matters to you?"

Wilf squinted his eyes the way he always did when he was being goaded into taking a stand. Normally he would never do such a thing with a total stranger, but this girl's scantily-clothed body and surly attitude were starting to bother him. Ph.D. or not, he'd tried to help her, and still she was as churlish as her filthy, moaning assistant.

"Age means nothing," he replied softly, "and I don't think it should. Clothing, on the other hand, or at least a modicum of modesty and self-restraint in its use, should be important to everyone—PhDs included."

Wilf didn't know what he expected the girl to say. But when she said nothing, merely regarding him in silence, he was surprised. At length she turned away.

"Have you had time to see much of Cornwall?" she asked abruptly.

"I've only been in England two days."

"And you are here in St. Martin because?"

Wilf shrugged and gave a self-effacing grin. "I was bored, so I decided to look around. This is where I ended up."

"You aren't staying here then? In St. Martin?"

"Between Looe and Polperro—with some friends."

"Polperro," Kerensa Tansin exclaimed scornfully. "A smuggler's haven, it was called three or four centuries ago. Now it is a lovely community—just lovely! Friends, you say? One would have thought they might encourage you to explore the coast, which is much more romantic than an out-of-the-way spot such as this. Penzance, now, isn't far from Polperro, at least by rail, and I think an uneducated Yank like you might enjoy it."

Stung by her perception, Wilf merely regarded her. "Uneducated?" he finally asked, determined to control the angry response that had come so quickly to his mind.

"Well, yes. With only two days in country, you are most certainly uneducated when it comes to British history and customs."

"Actually, that's true," Wilf admitted quietly. "For instance, I was surprised when I learned Penzance was in Cornwall." What he was saying to the young woman was the absolute truth, which his mother had always told him would never hurt anyone, himself most of all. In this case, however—

"I'd heard of the place, of course, but I had never associated it with England. I'd always assumed it was in Africa somewhere, maybe along the Barbary Coast."

"Don't say that too loudly around here." Kerensa had now tilted her head again, and was regarding him through the dark lenses of her glasses. "The locals are sensitive about their pirates, you see, and for less than that, you might end up in one of the old smuggler's caves and tunnels that still perforate the cliffs hereabouts. They say foreigners used to disappear into them all the time, and some still do!"

In an instant the woman's smile was back, exactly as if she had made no sort of threat at all. "Of a truth," she continued easily, "perhaps you are better off to stay inland. One has never seen such a pirate's town as Penzance, which even today is a perfect model for Gilbert and Sullivan's pirates. The place is filled with the modern sort, of course, hawking cheap and nasty trinkets that American tourists queue up to pay dear for. Even today, pirates in Penzance are tight as a fish's bum!"

"Well, this American tourist thanks you for the warning," Wilf drawled easily. "Only, I didn't catch why you and Orange-hair are here in this little out-of-the-way spot yourselves."

"Research," Kerensa replied simply, and then she turned abruptly away.

"Hey, hold up there! Hasn't anyone ever taught you manners? Polite folks don't walk away from others in the midst of a conversation!"

The girl stopped as if she had been slapped. Then slowly, very slowly, she turned back around. "Yes?" she questioned, her voice more icy than ever.

"Nothing, really." Wilf was seething as he started once again toward her, his irritation a palpable thing that he would not allow into his voice. That he kept controlled and calm. "I was just curious is all. Is your research centered here, down near Polperro, or where? Being somewhat of a student myself, I guess I'm mildly curious about the locations of some of these ancient sites."

"There are more than enough maps to show you all you wish to know!"

"Ah, yes." Wilf smiled with understanding, knowing full well that his expression was nothing more than a mask to cover his resentment over the girl's incredible arrogance and shameless immodesty. "I've actually looked at one or two, and have wondered briefly at the mysterious folk who built Stonehenge and other neolithic monuments, many of which I understand still remain here in Cornwall. Those people, of course, were wiped out by the primitive Celtic tribes, who were in turn beaten back by Julius Caesar and his Roman armies. The Romans built Bath and Hadrian's Wall, and also established their capital at a place called Londoninium. Which of these ancient peoples are you studying here in St. Martin?"

Wilf paused, almost laughing at the girl's puzzled expression. "Or are you perhaps doing research into the bar-barian tribes from Germany and Denmark who called themselves Angles and Saxons?" he continued. "They swept Rome off the southern end of your island between three and six hundred years after Christ, establishing Angle-land in the bargain. And of course Angle-land, in today's parlance, has been shortened to become England."

"Who are you?"

"Wilf Abbott fits me pretty well," Wilf grinned his dazzling but inofficious smile. "Or you can call me a reader if you'd like, for I am one. But now, Dr. Tansin, I have a question for you. My friends last evening told me there was some historical evidence for Robin Hood, whom I had always thought was fictional. To be honest, I have thought the same of King Arthur. Then I read quite recently where some also believe him to have been real. Since you are doing research in this area, do you have an opinion about the reality of the English king whom Walt Disney and Mark Twain have both made so famous?"

The girl's expression slowly relaxed from amazement into a slight smile. "Actually, Mr. Abbott, I do. I'm convinced he lived during the time of the Angles and Saxons you mentioned a moment ago, perhaps six hundred years after Christ, and was more than likely a Christianized Roman general who was fighting valiantly, but in vain, against the invading barbarians."

"Hmmm. Interesting hypothesis. Tintagel on the northern coast of Cornwall is promoted by the British Tourist Authority as Arthur's birthplace, and people by the thousands flock to see the ruins of his old castle. Unfortunately, that castle was built in the thirteenth century by somebody called the Earl of Cornwall, a Norman who traced his heritage back to the eleventh century Norman invader, William the Conqueror."

"Very good!" The girl smiled sweetly. "And now I *am* impressed. Truthfully, we don't know where the man we now call Arthur was born, though legend has it that the location of his birth was near those more modern ruins at Tintagel."

"I've never given much credence to legends."

"Perhaps you should. Exceptional deeds over the course of time become songs and legends, so it is certain that some good man from near Tintagel, carrying the name Arthur or some other, did many things wondrously well. Thus birth was given to the stories that your Walt Disney and Mark Twain, as well as a host of others, have profited from in the centuries since."

"Interesting thought. On Bodmin Moor, which according to the map is only a few dozen kilometers north of here, lies Dozmary Pool, where the man we call Arthur threw his sword *Excalibur* out to the Lady of the Lake. Or at least so the legends say. And only a little north of the pool, just outside of the town of Camelford but still on Bodmin Moor, is an innocuous little spot called Slaughter Bridge. It is said that is where Arthur met his sad end at the hands of the evil Medraut or Mordred—who was perhaps an Angle or Celtic warlord of the time?"

"You're asking me for confirmation?"

"Well," Wilf nodded,"it would be interesting to know what really happened on that lonely moor so many centuries past."

"Yes, it would," the girl agreed softly, her own mental weapons armed and ready once more. "But did you note the name of Camelford? As a student, you should have. There are those who swear it's the modern spelling for the ancient town of Camlann or Camelot, which some linguists agree also means ford or crossing over the River Camel, which of a truth flows nearby. So take a good thought, Wilford Abbott, before you cast aspersions on *any* of the dearly-held legends of we Englishfolk."

At her latest dig, Wilf's smiling mask spread again. "I'll do that," he murmured even while his eyes flashed his true emotions. "You have my word on it." Turning then, he glanced at the youth of the orange hair, who was now massaging his throat and trying to sit up. "If this woman fires you, friend Petroc, you'll be getting off lucky!"

Then, without a backward glance, and forgetting entirely that he had not yet entered the pub to purchase his coach ticket to Polperro, Wilf turned and walked away.

Chapter Nine

"*W*ell, Mr. Penryn, do you think you'll live?"

"I...I'll live," the youth rasped as he rubbed his terribly sore throat, "at least long enough to split the bloke in half!"

"Wilford Abbott? My but you are slow to learn! He could have killed you, you know. My recommendation, Petroc, is that you leave him well enough alone."

"Don't be funny!" Petroc was still rubbing his throat, and his voice was hardly more than a whisper. "Not in donkey's years, I won't run from him! You'll see. One of these days his smalls will be bunched for good, and I'll do the bunching!"

Kerensa Tansin chuckled. "Then I wish you luck, Mr. Penryn, for I'd say he is a dangerous man. Perhaps that is because his anger is so close to the surface. Obviously he was endeavoring to disguise it, but it was very evident in his voice. Other than that, what did you think of him?"

"Besides wanting to kill him, you mean?" Petroc's eyes were burning with his hatred. "Well, he ain't top hole, that's certain. As far as a physical, I'd say he's six foot and a bit more, weighs in at twelve stone, maybe a bit less, and ain't got much of his hair left, at least on top."

"Yes, yes! But him?"

"Daft!" Petroc growled.

"You're a fine help!" For a moment Kerensa did not move. A tipper lorry or dump truck rumbled past them on the road, and abruptly she smiled. "The next coach isn't through here until eight, or so the schedule says. Our American likely purchased a return ticket when he left Polperro, but in case he got a single because of his ignorance, why don't you queue up and buy another for him."

"Hello!" Petroc stormed angrily. "For the American?"

"That's right, Mr. Penryn. British hospitality, you know. If you'd like, get some bubble and squeak for yourself while you're about it. Proper pub food, that is."

"He might not even be taking the coach," Petroc growled with disgust, only partially mollified by the cold meat, cabbage and potatoes he would soon be eating. Of course he knew he could substitute for pasties and sweets without the woman knowing, and that made it a little better.

"True enough." Kerensa replied with a smile. "But no matter. Get the ticket anyway. By-the-by, Mr. Penryn, do *you* think what I wear is immodest?"

"Oiaye, no!" For the hundredth time that day Petroc looked lustfully at his new boss, whose scantily-covered figure was almost as enticing as the money she had so foolishly entrusted to his care. "What you're wearing is perfect for the sort of work you do! Keeps you cool in the sun, dries out fast after a rain. I'm telling you, Dr. Ren, the Yank's daft!"

"Yes," the anthropologist said softly as she turned away. "And you, my dear Petroc Penryn, are a randy young liar. You know, I do believe I've changed my mind. Give me my wallet, please, and I'll go buy the ticket!"

"But...that's the job you gave me."

"Yes, it was."

"And if I don't give it back?" the orange-haired youth sneered as he rose to his feet, no longer doubting the woman's implications.

Kerensa Tansin smiled. "Then I'll simply call out to the American. I can still hear his footsteps, you know, so he isn't far off. I'll tell him you attacked me. I'm certain he'd know just what to do!"

Wildly Petroc looked around. But the woman was right, and he knew it. Not only was Wilford Abbott still within earshot, but there was no doubt at all in the still-sore young man's mind that the American could do far worse to him than he had already done. Could, and no doubt would!

"Thank you," Kerensa smiled sweetly as she took the finally extended wallet. "You may keep the money you've already pilfered out of it, Petroc. That, instead of the hundred quid I mentioned earlier, shall be your final pay!"

"You mean—" Petroc blustered, feeling stunned that Kerensa Tansin had somehow sussed out his theft of a wad of her bills. "But I thought—"

"Which you shouldn't have, not in your present condition. Mr. Penryn, my dear, you are sacked! If you are not gone from here back to Liskeard by tonight, I shall see that the coppers know not only that you and your brother truly did rob the woman in Liskeard, but that with your silly little knife you have also attacked both the American and myself!"

"But...I didn't attack you!"

"You did if I say you did." Again Kerensa's sweet smile lit the afternoon. "Now, off with you, for the longer I am around you, the more polluted I feel!"

Once the fuming Petroc was gone, having been given a lift by a lorry headed for Liskeard, Kerensa carefully changed into a second outfit she always carried in her pack. Meanwhile she found herself wondering, of all things, if the American would approve of it. Certainly it was far less revealing than her top and shorts.

As she moved carefully along the verge of the road away from *The Copley Arms*, Kerensa could not stop thinking about Wilford Abbott—or more correctly, about what he had said. Modesty. Why had he brought up modesty? And what, exactly, did it mean to him? Oh, she knew that the dictionary defined modesty as humble or unassuming behavior, acting with propriety, and lacking excesses or pretensions of any sort. That covered a wide range of possibilities—extremely wide.

Yet there was no doubt in Kerensa's mind that the American had been referring specifically to her manner of dress—or undress, as Petroc would have quite happily put it. The thing was, she admitted candidly as she moved through the tall grass that bordered the road, she had been dressing that way on purpose, completely oblivious to the fact that it might actually be offensive.

Guiltily, she then recalled an intentional decision to appear and act risque, a decision that she and several of her teenage friends had made years before when they had thought to attract the one and only Mr. Right, whom each had spent so many hours giggling and daydreaming over.

Then had come college, and quickly Kerensa had become so thoroughly involved in her schooling and research, busily climbing one academic pillar after another, that men in general and Mr. Right in particular, had been relegated to a distant second place. Or perhaps even last place, if the truth were known. Her style and manner of covering her body, therefore, had of necessity evolved toward more genteel fashions—at least until the beginning of this most recent project.

But was the dream of a Mr. Right in her future truly dead? No longer was the young professor sure. Recently, and at the oddest moments, she had found herself contemplating marriage. This startled her, especially because for so long she had felt nothing—no matrimonial inclinations whatsoever! But now, she thought disgustedly, when she should have been in a position to make some wonderfully significant contributions to mankind, she was instead having unrealistic daydreams of marital bliss with some faceless caricature of a man who would somehow glide into her life and sweep her off her giddy feet!

Such nonsensical thinking distressed Kerensa deeply. But no matter how she tried to force it from her mind, for some reason it would not go. And now had come a perfect stranger into her life, a backwoods American cowboy, of all people, telling her with obvious sincerity that he found her choices distasteful, her entire being immodest! As if he had any right to say such things in the first place. Who on God's green earth did the man think he was?

In frustration, Kerensa shook her head, trying to clear it. This was insane! Why was she worrying about the opinions of some unknown cowboy when she was in the middle of what might turn out to be the most important work of her life? No! She had to refocus herself, to concentrate on her work—

Opinion! That's what it was! The upset American was merely expressing his opinion! Which opinion, she declared with fists clenched at her sides, was being given in anger and therefore mattered not at all!

But if it didn't matter, she reminded herself almost scornfully scant seconds later, then why was she unable to forget it? Why in this great wide world of incredibly diverse humanity was she feeling so decidedly uncomfortable about what one goofily clothed and decidedly unimportant American was thinking? Was it her pride that was hurt? Was she angry because he had not found her attractive?

Certainly most other men would not have agreed with him, which had been proven to her complete satisfaction again and again! Though Kerensa endeavored to pay no outward attention, she was very much aware of mens' gazes, and who could miss their inane whistles and catcalls? She had even known of young Petroc's randy stare, and he had thought he was being so sly!

Unfortunately, such knowledge did leave Kerensa in a dilemma. On the one hand, thoughts of the lust in mens' minds left her decidedly uncomfortable. When younger, she had not been able to imagine that the male species could think such things. Now that she was older and knew better, such facts troubled her deeply. On the other hand, she was flattered by the attention men gave her and was even empowered by it. People all about her claimed it to be a man's world, where women were second-class citizens. Kerensa thought otherwise, and for years had reveled in the degree to which her beauty—not her body but her beauty—had enabled her to obtain her desires.

The problem, she supposed, was that advancing age was bringing about a change in her thinking. During her post-doc research, the entire scenario of modern relationships between men and women had grown increasingly troublesome, though for the life of her she hadn't been able to determine why. All she knew was that, no matter where she looked or with whom she talked, something seemed to be lacking. Something, somewhere, was missing from her life.

Again Kerensa thought of the angry-voiced American. Perhaps he really did think her figure ugly. Or at the very least, unattractive. If so, then might he be gay? Was that the source of his anger? But no, that wasn't possible! She had been in the company of men with homosexual tendencies often enough to know they seemed to radiate a certain spirit—very discomforting, she found it—that was absolutely unmistakable. And there had been no such spirit about the American! Yet, what other reason might he have had for finding her unattractive?

No matter which way she searched, Kerensa could think of none, unless it was—and this was an amazingly revolutionary thought—that Wilford Abbott didn't find her unattractive at all! Might it rather be—and her mind was suddenly a-twitter with the possibility—that he found her *very* attractive? So much so, in fact, that her exposure was truly offensive to him? To his innate sensibilities? To his actual inner nature?

If that were true, her mind raced on, then what she had observed, for the first time in her adult life, she might add, was a man's personal sense of impropriety, his own belief- centered discomfort over the fact that a woman—any woman—was exposing herself excessively.

Of a truth she had never expected to find such a thing! She had not even supposed that such could exist in the mind or heart of man—at least a man of her generation! If it should turn out that it did, her mind thundered at her while she walked slowly forward into the late afternoon, then it might very likely become the most significant discovery she would ever make!

Only, Kerensa's reasoning screamed back at her with even more irony, now that she had gleefully attacked and upset the American so thoroughly, how would she ever know?

Though he hadn't really thought it through, Wilf had gone to Cornwall seeking happiness, which to him meant planning and then following what he fully expected would be a smooth and unopposed course to the attainment of exactly what he desired. Simple or complex, childish or mature, worldly or spiritual, selfish or selfless, legal or illegal, good or evil—Wilf and most of the rest of us want what we want, and we are convinced that happiness will come with it.

Interestingly, since our wants are constantly changing, despite what we might think at any given moment, few of us actually know what we want! Moreover, in this life there is no such thing as a smooth and unopposed course. There is always going to be opposition—unexpected curve-balls and detours and punches below the belt—all of which leave us gasping and swinging wildly and far, far from where we thought we were headed.

These things, so his story went, Wilf was about to learn....

Chapter Ten

*T*he sun was just dropping beyond the rugged Cornish Peninsula when a discouraged Wilf Abbott, utterly exhausted from his fruitless search, as well as two days and nights with almost no rest, walked away from the last house on the winding country lane.

Who was she? Who in heaven's name, he was asking himself over and over, was the girl at the crossing? *And what had she been doing there?*

Painstakingly, Wilf had gone door-to-door, approaching virtually every house on both sides of the river that seemed even remotely close enough to have something to do with his mystery. Though none of the people he had spoken with had known anything of the lovely schoolgirl he was describing, several claimed to have seen her in the past few days. Presenting herself at their doorsteps just as Wilf had been doing, she had asked only if she had been known to them, or if perhaps she might have stayed with them during some previous tenure.

Which was crazy on the face of it, Wilf thought. If anyone would have known such a thing, it should have been her! That she apparently didn't, was troubling in the extreme.

Might she have been suffering from amnesia? Or was she perhaps a mental case, a teenager burned out on drugs or something similar that had brought on a form of dementia? Or maybe she was nothing more than part of a juvenile prank, a silly schoolgirl out on a dare, doing a thing that others of her childish mentality thought hilarious.

Of course, Wilf had no idea which of his three possibilities might prove correct. Perhaps none of them would. Nevertheless, everything—virtually every single thing he knew of the girl, which admittedly was hardly anything at all—led him to believe one of the latter two scenarios. The first, amnesia, remained a distant posibility, but it *was* distant, and was something he was loath to consider.

Being juvenile, on the other hand, made more sense. So many modern kids were out of their minds with illicit drug use, which he knew was epidemic the world over. And they were just as out of their minds with immaturity! Babies in big bodies was how his brother Brig described them, the bizzare Petroc and his brother Neville being prime examples. In fact, if it hadn't been for what had passed between Wilf and the girl at the crossing the evening before, the immaturity factor alone would have been reason enough to dismiss her.

But there remained that blasted, magical communication—

Glancing at the setting sun, Wilf subconsciously reached into his shirt pocket to check on his coach ticket and for the first time realized that he had forgotten to purchase one. Doggone arrogant woman, he thought, with her irritating way of getting to him! She'd upset him so thoroughly that he'd entirely forgotten to go into the blasted pub!

Disgustedly Wilf glanced off into the trees. Normally he'd have turned and followed the winding road back the way he had come. But with evening approaching, and the coach arriving from the north who knew when, he was feeling a growing sense of urgency. Despite that he was certain he would be trespassing through yards and perhaps even estates, he had to get down to that pub before it closed! Besides, he thought with a half grin, for an Arizona country boy like himself, striking out through an unknown countryside was a perfectly normal thing to do!

Still, his hyperactive conscience reminded him as he moved easily and practically silently over the edge of the bluff and down the steep slope, this *was* trespassing. Worse, it was entirely his fault that he felt forced into doing it. If it hadn't been for his pride and tragic temper, which seemed always and forever to be connected, he'd never have allowed the anthropologist to get to him in the first place. Would he never learn, he found himself wondering as he slid and scrambled down through the trees? Would he never overcome his foolish anger?

At the bottom of the bluff, Wilf started along the road toward the distant pub, which was already ablaze with light. Would he be on time? Or had the last coach of the night already passed by? If so, then he'd end up stuck for the night in the nothingness of St. Martin, which he did not for a moment relish. Of course he'd spent plenty of other nights sleeping at the side of some nameless road, particularly in South America, and so he knew he would survive. What worried him, though, were Clive and Ann Payne. They'd naturally be concerned.

Blast! Why had he become involved with that doggone anthropologist woman, anyway? It would have been so simple to have just walked away. For years he'd made it a practice to leave people alone, merely mirthfully observing as they stewed themselves silly in their own juices. Only occasionally had he ever become involved, and every time it had been to his own deep regret.

This, Wilf could see already, was going to be no exception. He'd allowed himself to become involved, his pride and temper had tripped him up, and now here he was—in deep doodoo! Let the woman run around half clothed or even completely naked if that was what she wanted! So what? Why did it have to be an issue with him? Just because his mother had so thoroughly ingrained her sense of modesty and propriety into his brain didn't mean he had to go around forcing it onto others!

After all, he hadn't been forced to look at her. He hadn't even been forced to speak with her. For a fact, he should have done neither! And without doubt he should have turned away at the first intimation of trouble within himself—at the first welling up of desire that had quickly become disgust, not alone at the woman's pathetic immodesty but at her intellectual arrogance. That he had not, was his own stupid fault!

The thing was, she had ambushed him—caught him off guard with her frank and open handshake and self-introduction. Besides which, he thought ruefully, she had not been half-bad looking, at least in a strange and grimy sort of way—

A train whistle made Wilf pause, and as he turned automatically toward the sound, he was astounded to see that he had come again to the intersection that led to the unmarked crossing. Moreover, the one-coach train had also reached the crossing, and was just drawing to its proper halt behind the sign, no doubt making the same final run of the day he had taken from Liskeard just twenty-four hours before.

For an instant, Wilf felt as though he were living in a dream, a strange warp of time where far too much was happening. Then he saw her, and everything around him seemed to stop! The girl, dressed in the same school uniform he had seen twice before, was standing almost exactly as she had been standing the previous evening, the only difference being that this time she was on the far side of the tracks. Still, her arms were wrapped around her just as they had been the night before, and her face was turned toward the oncoming train. But despite the fact that she was profiled rather than facing directly toward him, Wilf could see the girl clearly enough in the waning light to feel certain it was her.

For the third time in twenty-four hours, Wilf was seeing the girl with the incredibly deep blue eyes.

His heart again pounding, Wilf crossed the empty road and started toward her, intent only on her lovely visage. Surely she would see him coming, he thought! But she did not look at him, apparently did not even notice him. Instead the train had her full and complete attention, so that Wilf found himself wondering, as he strode forward, if she might be waiting for someone.

Quickly he approached the tracks, the train outside his line of sight but starting forward again, moving into the crossing.

In fact, it was moving much more rapidly than he had supposed it could, and with a start Wilf realized it was going to cut off his view of the unknown girl. And in the same instant of that realization, Wilf was dumbfounded to see her step forward, exactly as if she were about to cast herself beneath the iron wheels of the train.

"Hey, you!" he yelled at the top of his lungs, frantically trying to make himself heard above the diesel engine. "Stand back, girl! Get back from the tracks!"

As though on a swivel, the girl's head spun toward him, her eyes widened perceptibly, and her look of confusion was replaced in an instant with one of startled recognition. Less than a heartbeat later that same incredible communication passed from her startlingly blue eyes into his own, and then—

With an almost deafening whistle of warning, the train passed into the crossing, cutting off Wilf's view of the girl. Fifteen seconds it took the single car to pass by, no longer, he was certain. Then silence descended onto the roadway where it crossed the tracks, almost an eerie silence, and Wilf found himself staring westward across the rails and toward the river in dumbfounded amazement.

There was no one there!

No one at all!

In three long strides, he was across the tracks and frantically looking around, peering anywhere a person might possibly be hiding. But it didn't matter where he looked, or even how long he spent doing it. In fact, from the get-go he'd had the numbing feeling that it wouldn't. Somehow, in that short fraction of a minute while the train had been between them, just as she had disappeared that morning from in front of the pasty shop in Polperro, the unknown girl had managed somehow to vanish from the crossing. Exactly as if she were a ghost, or some very troubled spirit!

And Wilford Abbott, his mind whirling with the impossibility of it all, had no earthly idea of what to do next.

Chapter Eleven

*I*t was dusk again, a day later, and Wilf was back at the crossing. Only this time he was not taking chances. Instead of being on the road, he was beside it, hidden behind a tree and some shrubs so that he could observe without being seen. Of course, hiding in such a way made him feel guilty, at least a little. But discovering the identity of the young woman had become paramount to him—so important, in fact, that his entire future seemed to hang on it!

The trouble was, this evening she hadn't come. Either that, or else the train was running late, and she had become aware of it. It was already darker than it had been the evening before, and yet there had been no sign of her, no indication that she was even in the vicinity of the crossing.

In the distance, Wilf heard the familiar whistle, and briefly he smiled. At least, he thought as he repositioned himself for greater comfort, the train would arrive before full dark. Now if only the unknown schoolgirl would show up!

Something—a slight noise, perhaps—distracted Wilf so that he turned away from the crossing. Seeing nothing he turned back, and was dumbfounded to discover the girl standing a few feet back from the rails, just as if she had been waiting there for hours! That was not possible, of course. It couldn't have happened! Only—

The train was drawing nearer; Wilf could hear it approaching from behind him. Yet his eyes never left the girl on the roadway. She was standing slightly turned so he could not quite see her face, but he was certain it was her. It had to be! Her sheen of dark hair cascaded around her shoulders, even in profile her lovely face was radiant, and of course the uniform of British schoolgirls was as it had always been.

Wilf was captivated! Moreover, he was immobilized so that he could not have moved even if movement had been his single greatest desire. All he could do was stare from his fortunate hiding place, devouring the girl's beauty with his eyes while the rest of him ached to touch her, to hold her close, and never allow her to get away—

The close sounding of the train's whistle startled Wilf just as it had the night before. Somehow the train had already stopped, and now it started again, pounding past him and into the crossing, and in that same instant Wilf's joy was turned to fear. As she had the evening before, the unknown girl had taken a deliberate step toward the tracks. And then, as Wilf looked on, she took another.

Terrified, he leaped to his feet, his hands raised in futile protest while his voice bellowed a strident warning that no shrieking whistle could possibly cover. Yet she could not hear! For some reason the lovely but unknown girl could not hear his warning! Instead she seemed mesmerized by the turning wheels of the oncoming train, almost as if they were calling out to her—

Frantically, Wilf lunged from his hiding place and toward the narrow road. He was still yelling, still trying by force of sheer will to hold the girl back, to stop her. Yet his pace seemed abysmally slow, his shouting as if it were in a vacuum. Nothing was reaching the girl, nothing at all that had anything to do with him—

To his horror, Wilf watched as she seemed to stumble. Then her hands came up in a frantic effort to catch herself, she failed, and a scant second later he watched her pitch forward onto her lovely face just in front of the rear double wheels of the branch-line special.

There was an almost imperceptible bump, no more, and then Wilf was screaming out his horror and agony of spirit—

"Wilford? Wilford? Are you all right?"

"I...uh...I'm fine. Wh...what's happening?"

"You were screaming awfully." Ann Payne sat down on the side of his bed. "It was a frightful nightmare, was it?"

Dumbly Wilf nodded, still trying to understand that it had been only a dream—still struggling to unscramble the meaning of it, but making very little progress.

"Something from your past, was it?"

Feeling more than a little bewildered, Wilf shook his head. "No, not from my past. Maybe from my future, though I'm not sure."

"Was it the girl? Morwenna Miller? Are you dreaming of her, then?"

With a sigh, Wilf plopped his head back onto the pillow. He was so tired, so incredibly tired, and the previous few hours had done him no good whatsoever. After wandering about the crossing for an hour or so, wearing himself out with stewing and fretting, as his sister Annie liked to put it, but not once catching another glimpse of Morwenna Miller, he'd gone to the pub only to discover that he'd missed the last coach. Then had come another tedious wait, until finally a friendly little fellow at the pub had given him a lift into Looe. There he'd caught a cab out to Trelawne Cross and the bungalow at Granite Henge, where he'd found that Clive and Ann had already retired, no doubt worrying about him all the while. Now this crazy nightmare had made things worse than ever!

"I'm sorry to disturb you and Clive, Ann. Really, I am!"

"Hush, Wilford. You've nothing to apologize for. Besides, Clive sleeps so deeply he's sure to miss Gabriel's trumpet announcing the Second Coming, and will end up having to snore another thousand years."

Despite his anxiety, Wilf chuckled.

"Now, was it Morwenna Miller you were dreaming about?"

"It was," Wilf admitted miserably. "I...I think I saw her die."

"If it was under the wheels of the train at Terras Bridge, then you most certainly did."

"Terras Bridge?" Wilf breathed, not yet acknowledging the last of Ann's statement. "The crossing has a name?"

"Not the crossing, Wilford, just the bridge. I thought Clive told you. He found it today—or I suppose it is now yesterday—on an Ordinance Survey map of St. Austell and Liskeard."

Slowly Wilf shook his head. "He didn't tell me. In fact, I haven't seen him since the two of you dropped me off."

Rolling her eyes, Ann tapped her forehead with the palm of her hand. "That's right, Wilford! Goodness! They say that memory is the first to go, and they must have been thinking of me when they said it. As a matter of fact, Clive spent two or three hours helping one of the other guests here, so I know he couldn't have told you!"

"It's all right, Ann," Wilf smiled. "How...did you know what I saw in my dream—how the girl died, I mean?"

"Morwenna Miller?" Ann sighed deeply. "Because it happened exactly like that, Wilford, ten years ago almost to the day! Apparently she was waiting for the train at that crossing. Jeanette Fellick, who with her husband David owns these bungalows, tells me the child took a cab to that very place at the same time every single day!"

"Wait a minute, Ann. How does Mrs. Fellick know that?"

"Morwenna Miller was one of the Granite Henge guests, Wilford. She was staying in another of these very cottages—had been for two or three weeks when the terrible tragedy occurred."

"Perhaps I might have a visit with Mrs. Fellick?"

"She'd love to meet you! I've already told her about you, and she's thrilled to have a handsome young American as her guest. I also mentioned your interest in Morwenna Miller, the poor dear. She was only a child, too—had hardly even passed her 'A' Levels and got out of school. That's why it was such a mystery! Why would a young thing like that, with everything in the world to live for, take her own life in such a horrible, horrible manner?"

"She didn't commit suicide, Ann," Wilf responded with a sense of wonder that he had dreamed such a thing. "The train's wheels must have hypnotized her or something. It looked to me like that was what made her stumble. Then when she tried to catch herself it was too late—too everlastingly late—for either of us!"

"Oh, Wilford dear, I am so sorry!"

Bleakly, Wilf looked up at the kind woman. "So am I, Ann. But more than sorry, I am confused! I really am! What's the point of all this? Why should I keep seeing the ghost of a girl ten years dead? Worse than that, why should I keep experiencing an incredible silent communication each time I see her—a sense that there is something glorious and wonderful between us that seems exactly like what existed between you and Clive more than half a century ago!"

Instant tears started from Ann's eyes. "I...I had no idea this was happening."

"Yeah," Wilf growled in utter frustration, "and I wish it wasn't! Do you know that it even happened in my dream—my nightmare! No fooling, Ann! Just like Clive, that look in her eyes made me feel like I had finally come home! Well, that's crazy! Insane!"

"What...what will you do about it, Wilford?"

"Do?" Wilf smiled wryly. "For starters, I'll go back to sleep and get a little much needed rest—and give you some, too. Then in the morning, well, as we've been speaking I've been lying here making up my mind. With daylight, Ann, I'm out of here, off to explore a little more of merry olde England!"

"But, what about Jeanette Fellick?"

"Oh, that's right!" For a moment Wilf felt trapped, as though no matter how he endeavored to flee, unseen forces continued to suck him back into the real-life nightmare his life had become. Still, he knew how badly Ann wanted him to meet Mrs. Fellick, and it seemed that Mrs. Fellick was just as anxious to meet him. Besides, it shouldn't take more than an extra hour or so—

"You see, Ann?" Wilf grinned disarmingly. "My memory's worse than yours, and I'm at least a little bit younger. Very well, I'll speak with Mrs. Fellick first thing, and *then* I'm out of here!"

"Do you understand what leaving means, my dear?"

"Yeah," Wilf declared as he tenderly patted Ann's soft hand, "it means, when all is said and done, that I'm choosing not to be nuts! Because right now, nuts is what it feels like I've become!"

"Actually, Wilford, it means none of us will ever know."

"Yeah, that, too. And maybe, Ann, just maybe, that's exactly how it should be."

Chapter Twelve

"Good morning. Are you Mrs. Fellick?"

For some time, Wilf had been seated by the pool enjoying the misty rain, waiting for the Granite Henge office to open. Now that it had, he wanted to get this interview over with as quickly as possible. He doubted that he would learn anything new about the girl called Morwenna Miller, but it wouldn't make any difference if he did. His decision to leave was final, and he would visit with Mrs. Fellick only as a courtesy to both her and Ann.

"Yes," the woman behind the desk replied with a quick smile, "I'm Jeanette Fellick. This is my husband, David. And you must be the American guest of Clive and Ann Payne. My goodness! You are a hero, you know, saving Ann's purse from those awful young men up in Liskeard. She's told me of it twice now, and everyone else who will listen. In fact, it is Wilford, isn't it? Wilford Abbott?"

"Yes, ma'am, it is."

Jeanette Fellick, now that Wilf had a moment to observe her, was a smiling, youngish looking woman, very thin, with quick, nervous movements and long reddish-blonde hair that flowed halfway down her back. Her well-mannered husband David, who had been standing behind her at the desk, was lean but more solid looking, with graying hair, trimmed beard, and a short pony-tail. His gnarled hands, Wilf thought, were more the hands of a carpenter or fisherman than they were the proprietor of some holiday bungalows.

"Oh, David," Jeanette exclaimed with a happy laugh, "see how polite he is? Just like Ann told us. Well, Wilford, when I heard of all you had done, I utterly refused money for your stay! No, I said to Ann, I will not take a single shilling! You are welcome to stay as long as you wish."

Wilf smiled. "That's very good of you, Mrs. Fellick, and I thank you sincerely. Actually, though, my intention is to be gone within the hour."

"Oh, dear! I am sorry to hear that, really I am."

"Well, I've already been here longer than I anticipated, and folks tell me there's a great deal more to Great Britain than this small corner of Cornwall."

"Yes, there is more," David Fellick said, speaking for the first time, "but none that is better. For years I fished out of other ports, but you can bet I've thrown out my last anchor, Wilford. Cornwall is where I intend to stay."

"Good for you, sir," Wilf smiled. "And I hope one day to die in Arizona, for I feel the same about it. Now, Mrs. Fellick, Ann and I were discussing a young woman who apparently died at a crossing near Looe, and Ann said that you—"

"Please call me Jeanette, Wilford. I like that so much better."

"Very well, Jeanette. Is there anything either you or your husband—David, I mean—can tell me about her?"

"Right. Well, both of us remember her clearly. That's certain! Her death was a terrible tragedy, just terrible! Such a sweet young thing; rented the bungalow for a month and was only here three weeks before she killed herself. Alone the whole time, too, which was a bit curious."

"What do you mean?"

"Well, it's unusual to have such a young person on holiday completely on their own."

"Right, right," David quickly added. "We let our bungalows to single people quite often, but not to one so young.

We were new here then—had just bought the place a year or two before—or we might have been more up on what was happening."

"Learning does seem to take time, for all of us. Do you happen to recall her name?"

"I should," Jeanette responded, "the way folks keep ringing us up to talk about her, the poor child. It amazes me of late how many people are seeing her ghost, particularly when there hasn't been a single sighting in the past ten years, at least that I know of. Now she seems to be everywhere!"

Jeanette smiled apologetically. "But I digress, Wilford, and I apologize. Her name was Morwenna Miller. She never gave us any middle name or her home address, at least that I recall; just forwarded us a deposit and then showed up here with hundreds of pounds in travelers cheques, which she used to pay in advance."

"You've had others inquire about her more than once?" Wilf pressed.

"Besides all these recent inquiries, at least once a year a news reporter from Liskeard will make an inquiry, as if I should know if her body's ever been claimed."

"Viv Twornicki, the reporter is," David Fellick nodded. "I see her frequently at the newspaper offices on Great Place in Liskeard. I pass by there on my way to therapy."

"Right," Jeanette continued almost impatiently. "Morwenna Miller's buried at Talland Church, you know. Not in the churchyard itself, I suppose because she was a suicide, but just outside, overlooking Talland Bay."

"Actually," David interjected quietly, "I believe the graveyard was simply too full. After all, the church has been there since sometime before 1199, when they have record of their first vicar, a fellow named John Gervays. One can only imagine how many people in the Talland parish have been buried in the churchyard since then. Even the walkways are lined with old headstones."

"Right," Jeanette agreed again, smiling up at her husband. Then she turned back to Wilf. "It's a lovely place, so peaceful.

I go there at every opportunity! Anyway, I've been too trusting with reporters, I can tell you that. Not Viv, mind you, but the ones from Plymouth, St. Austell, and Truro. I've lent them every last thing the poor child left behind that the police didn't confiscate, and none of it's ever been returned!"

"Items like clothing, you mean?"

"Right, though the police took most of that, as they did her handbag, travelers cheques—you know, the important things. But there were some personal items they didn't take—makeup, brushes for her hair—that sort of thing. She had the most beautiful hair, Wilford. Thick and dark, almost black, with a natural curl so that it cascaded down in the most lovely way over her shoulders. And her eyes? Such a clear, pure blue! Striking, they were!"

"I...can imagine," Wilf responded quietly.

"Anyway, it's gone; all of it. Now, even if you wanted, I have nothing of the poor girl's left to give you."

"Well, I don't really need anything, but thank you anyway. Do you recollect anything else about her?"

Soberly the woman shook her head. "I'm afraid I don't. David and I were in a terrible car accident a year or so back, and since then I've had an awful time with my memory."

"I'm sorry to hear that," Wilf murmured, thinking for a moment of his own terrible losses.

"Well, it's been a hard struggle, for both of us. I don't remember very well, and as he mentioned, nearly every day David has to drive into Liskeard for therapy. Otherwise his back gets so bad he can't do a thing. But at last we're doing a little better, for which we thank the good Lord every blessed day!"

"That's good," Wilf responded sincerely. "Uh...was Morwenna Miller by chance a schoolgirl? Ann says so."

Jeanette smiled radiantly. "Why, yes, now that you mention it, she was! If I'm not mistaken, she'd just passed her 'A' Levels at a public school up north somewhere and seemed quite proud of herself. No, wait! That may have been a girl who stayed here last year—with her parents, of course. One thing about Morwenna Miller that I do recollect, though; she might have been on holiday, but she never watched the telly, not ever. She liked the radio, but that was all. We used to charge extra for the telly, so that's how I know. She never even had David put one in her bungalow. Oh, and another thing! Not once did I ever see her leave in one of the host of taxis I was forever calling for her, when she was out of her school uniform— including the blazer!"

"Is that unusual?"

The happy woman laughed lightly. "For young people on holiday? Very unusual! Especially if it's warm, which I seem to recall, it was."

"Unlike today," Wilf groused under his breath.

"She didn't wear her uniform about our place, though," David interjected. "Jeanette doesn't recall this, apparently, but it was her opinion at the time that the child hardly wore anything at all."

"I do so recall," Jeanette glared up at her husband, her smile instantly gone. Then she turned back to Wilf. "And I must say, Wilford, attired in that manner, she looked anything but a child! In spite of the fact that it was her swimming attire, she wore it rain or shine, day and night, whenever she was here. It was an appalling display! Shocking!"

Doing his best not to chuckle, Wilf nodded. "I think I understand. Might I ask which newspaper it is that calls you?"

"Calls? Oh, you mean rings us up on the telephone! Why, Viv's paper—the same that first printed the story of her death. It's called *The Cornish Times*—a weekly, published in Liskeard. Viv gives us a ring, and so does that nice policeman who came out from Looe to investigate—the one who took her things. Even though he's no longer employed in Looe, sometimes he still rings us up two or three times a year!"

"Now, Wilford, will there be anything else?"

"Not that I know of." Wilf smiled and reached out, shaking hands with both of them. "Thank you both for your time. And thank you, too, for the wonderful stay. If I'm ever back in England and particularly Cornwall, you can bet I'll throw out my anchor here at your bungalows and nowhere else!"

Jeanette again laughed delightedly, David smiled, and Wilf walked out of the office and into the misty rain. And he was thinking, as he headed back to the Payne's bungalow, that now he was as informed regarding Morwenna Miller as he was ever going to be.

Chapter Thirteen

"*W*hy, Wilford Abbott, good morning! This is certainly a surprise!"

Stunned to see the admittedly lovely social anthropologist seated beside the pool, Wilf nearly groaned aloud. Lovely or not, he fervently wished that he would stop running into this obnoxious woman!

"Good morning, Dr. Tansin," he replied cooly. "I see you are out early to enjoy the rain."

"Oh, this isn't rain, not really. It's a spitting mist, I suppose we Brits would call it. It does little damage, but seems to come from every direction at once. Umbrellas are useless against it, as are caps such as I wear."

The strange woman was wearing her cap, all right—exactly the same as the day before—with her hair bunched up under it. Wilf had already noted that, as he had noted also the same wrap-around dark glasses. Today, however, she was fully and modestly clothed, no doubt due to the dramatic change in the weather.

"What are you doing here?" he asked, probably far too abruptly.

Kerensa's smile immediately vanished. "I was about to ask you the same thing. Is there some reason why you have been following me?"

Wilf almost laughed. "Me following you? Lady, you'd be

the last person I'd want to follow!"

Kerensa Tansin didn't back down. "Then who are you, and why is it you always appear where I happen to be?"

"Well," Wilf drawled, knowing this woman was getting to him again but no longer much caring, "not that it is any of your business, but I'm here because here is where I have stayed the past two nights. As I told you yesterday, my name is Wilford Abbott, though most folks call me Wilf. I am from Arizona, USA, and I am exactly what I told you—a reader and a student, though not very much of either one."

"And nothing else?"

Carefully, Wilf looked down at her. "Why do you ask that?"

"Because you also seem to be a searcher—a man looking for something that I am beginning to suspect may have to do with me."

Surprised, Wilf reached up and rubbed the stubble on his face and chin. "Interesting idea. How did you come to it?"

"Because you are here, and you...well, yesterday you were at *The Copley Arms!*"

"Mere coincidence," Wilf chuckled as he settled himself onto another of the wet lounge chairs. "Though I will admit that I had begun wondering the same about you—for the same reason."

"Then," Kerensa pressed quickly, "you aren't looking for something? At least from me?"

Shaking his head, Wilf regarded the highly-educated social anthropologist. "Oh," he replied solemnly, knowing he would be leaving as soon as Clive returned and that his reply really wouldn't matter, "I'm looking for something, all right. Unfortunately it's a search I've been conducting for most of my adult life. Recently it has taken a rather bizarre turn which I have been trying to grope my way through but which has only grown more dark and impenetrable. Consequently, I am abandoning it altogether. But I tell you in all sincerity, Dr. Kerensa Tansin, my search has nothing to do with you!"

"If that's so," Kerensa came back, her voice every bit as low and sincere as Wilf's, "and if you haven't intentionally sought me out, then why on earth should you care whether or not I am being modest—in whatever way you might have meant it?"

And then silently Kerensa sat, her hidden gaze fixed upon the suddenly cautious Wilford Abbott, waiting for his answer.

Apologies, Wilf said he learned the hard way while he was in Cornwall, are like apples and used cars. The more shiny and gussied up they are, the more obvious it is that somebody's trying to sell something....

Chapter Fourteen

"*T*hat...uh...that was a mistake."

"Yes, it was!"

"No," Wilf stumbled, "I mean, well, I don't even know why I said it, except that I was upset! How you dress or undress is none of my business, and I apologize for offending you."

"Nevertheless," Kerensa continued, apparently enjoying herself, "you were worried about what I was wearing. Yes, or no."

"I wasn't worried! I just...well, so much exposure made me uncomfortable, that's all."

"Are you saying that your discomfort was my fault?"

Wilf was amazed by this sudden attack, though he couldn't think of a good way out of it. "Not really," he admitted grudgingly. "In fact, I'm not saying that at all. The fault was entirely my own. *I* made me uncomfortable. Is that better? What you were displaying of your body was so appealing that I wanted to look again, to see more—which I believe was an entirely inappropriate and selfish response. That's why I just apologized!"

"So, you are admitting to lusting after me."

"Yeah," Wilf murmured, growing more uncomfortable by the moment. "I guess so."

"Nevertheless, you still feel that your lusting, which might be defined as your initially unrestrained desire for your own sexual gratification at my expense, was exacerbated, if not brought about entirely, by my immodest attire."

"That makes me sound lower than pond scum," Wilf admitted. "But yes, you've pegged my feelings regarding the moment about right. Still, I should have controlled my tongue better than I did, and I am sorry for not having done so."

"And so you do or don't think it's immodest for a woman— a person of either sex, actually—to go around mostly unclothed? Which is it?"

"What I think doesn't matter!" Wilf growled in frustration. "Look, lady, in the last two minutes you've pretty much cut me open and flayed me alive! I don't know what else you want, but as far as I'm concerned, we're through here! My apology is simple but sincere, and it'll have to be good enough!"

Wilf took a deep breath. "Now I'll go my way, you go yours, hopefully we'll never see each other again, and from this moment for the rest of forever, I'll keep on trying to be who my mother raised me to be, and you can wear or not wear any doggone thing you want!"

Abruptly Kerensa laughed, and Wilf was startled by the musical sound of it. "Don't be upset with me, Wilford Abbott. I'm not angry with you, and I'm not attacking you, either one."

"Yeah, right!"

"All right, then, I was attacking, just as you attacked Petroc yesterday. In many cases, it is the best form of defense. And now it's my turn to apologize to you. But I truly did wish to understand the reasons behind your accusations."

"Why?" Wilf groused, only partly mollified. "So you could sue me?"

Again the woman laughed delightedly. "Not at all. Besides that you're seeing the scientific side of me coming out through my questions, I've also learned the hard way that I must be careful of everyone. There is always someone trying to tear me down so they can use me for a stepping stone toward further- ing their own career."

"Well, you can relax about me!"

"Perhaps, though to my regret I've believed such statements before."

Wilf eyed the young woman. "You're that prominent, then?"

"I'm afraid so, at least in certain very limited circles."

"Interesting." Wilf paused, then smiled sincerely. "Well, Dr. Kerensa Tansin, if we'd met today instead of yesterday, I would never have accused you of immodesty in the first place. In spite of the rain and that silly baseball cap, I think you look nice today."

"Why, thank you, Wilford Abbott. That sounds very sincere."

"That's because I am being motivated by the most lofty of thoughts."

Kerensa Tansin smiled. "Yes, I believe that, and it pleases me. But back to the subject of my immodest attire. I've thought a great deal about what you accused me of and, as you see, I have done my best to respond to it."

"You dressed this way on account of me?"

Kerensa laughed again. "In a roundabout way, yes, though the weather helped my decision. Nevertheless, what you said had a definite effect. As I mentioned yesterday, professionally I study trends in people, specifically our particular generation. I have long been aware that we seem to be drifting, shedding our parents' and even more our grandparents' values as we search for our own identity. This is all well and good, I suppose—or at least scientifically it seems normal. The problem it creates for me is that I am personally uncomfortable with the direction our drifting seems to be taking us."

"Meaning?"

Kerensa sighed. "Meaning that I think we are becoming a very unlikable generation."

"Friend Petroc being a prime example, I hope, rather than myself?"

"Yes," Kerensa laughed, "Petroc, definitely, and before you had gone a hundred yards he was sacked and out of my life!"

"Smart move."

"I think so, though the poor boy is by no means alone in being unlikable. By and large our entire generation has become hedonistic, selfish and self-centered, and arrogant beyond imagination. In other words, we allow our lusts to drive and control us. In doing so, we are convinced we are following the only path to true happiness, and scorn all who attempt to tell us otherwise. Yet none of us are very happy. Most, in fact, are simply miserable."

Intrigued, Wilford was giving the anthropologist his full attention. He'd thought his parents—his mother in particular—were the only ones in all the world who'd advocated old, traditional values. Then he'd met the Paynes and discovered that they espoused the same beliefs. But here was an apparently well-respected British scientist who might be supporting the same ideas.

"I think," Kerensa was continuing, "that this shifting from happiness to misery—from natural concern for others to being consumed with our own selfish lusts or appetites—is most aptly illustrated by the way we are currently approaching the role of sexual union in our lives. For untold generations, human reproduction has been considered sacred, something to be zealously protected and confined to appropriate and well-defined relationships. Yes, there has always been a fringe element who lived outside these rules and mores, making sexual activity a business, if you will. But throughout history they have been only that—a very narrow fringe.

"Today, and I believe this to my own personal sorrow, the opposite is true. The modern fringe—and until yesterday I was not even sure my generation had one—are those who still maintain traditional, and very personal, values. To the rest of us, Wilford, integrity means whatever we want it to mean at the moment. Charity has become nothing more than token-giving to the pesky Salvation Army bell-ringer during the Christmas rush. We cannot build prisons fast enough to facilitate our accelerating need. Crime, divorce, abortion, and previously abhorrent alternate lifestyles that now scream for acceptance, illustrate that nothing is more important than our own self-gratification. Money is the ultimate reward of all our efforts. And promiscuous sex, in all of its ugly manifestations, has become perhaps the biggest business in the world."

For a long moment Kerensa stared off into the distance, her thoughts obviously elsewhere. Wilf, intrigued by the woman's observations, now found himself hoping that Clive would take a little longer—

"Disillusioned with all of this," the anthropologist continued abruptly, "I have for the most part withdrawn from the world. Losing myself in my work, I have at the same time disdainfully thumbed my nose at everything and everyone around me, doing nothing to improve matters because I believed nothing could be done. Then yesterday you took a stand on a completely traditional value—against me, of all persons—and my eyes began to open!"

Again Kerensa smiled. "Yes, Wilford Abbott, there is most definitely a fringe of goodness left in our generation, a fringe of at least one man who recognizes his human weakness for what it is and is doing his best to overcome it—one man whom I have now had the delightful privilege of meeting personally!"

Chapter Fifteen

*I*n amazement, Wilf stared at the girl—no, woman, he was now thinking—

"Unless I have missed something," Kerensa continued, "and I hope you will tell me if I have, you accused me of immodesty for no other reason than because it was true. I was dressed shamefully. Stated as succinctly as I am able, the sight of my immodesty made you uncomfortable because of what it brought out in you, which has far more to do with your own system of values than it does my near nakedness. Am I right?"

"I...I don't know."

"Very well," Kerensa smiled patiently. "The only other reasons you might have had, at least that I can think of, are that you found me unattractive beyond belief or that you are homosexual. Are either of these true?"

Now Wilf chuckled. "Hardly!"

"I thought not. Can you give me another explanation, then? One I may have missed?"

"I...uh...I don't think so," Wilf stammered. "Only, I think you are giving me credit where none is due."

"Why is that?"

"Well," Wilf responded, taking a deep breath and then plunging in, "maybe I believe as you say I do. In fact, I guess I do. But that doesn't mean I like it! I believe the way I do because it's how I was taught to believe! In fact, I can't tell you how many times I've cussed my mother for planting her quote-unquote 'value system' so deeply—not only her values but her smallest and most silly beliefs—her expectations, even, for the future. I've been stifled by them for years, yet I can't seem to get past them, at least not with any degree of comfort."

"Have you discussed this with her?"

"I can't," Wilf responded bitterly. "She and my dad are dead."

"I'm sorry."

"Yeah," Wilf smiled without mirth, "me, too. Mom was a determined woman who with every breath raised her children to cherish her outmoded virtues of integrity, charity, fidelity, and chastity. Of course growing up on our small and very rural ranch, which provided my folks with little more than a way to keep Mother and the rest of us hard at work while my father earned a living traveling to distant cities as a corporate executive, made it easy for us to believe such attitudes were universal. As you've discovered, they are not. But by the time of my parents' fatal accident, the mindset of my two living sisters and four brothers, as well as my own, obviously, had been firmly established."

"It must have been wonderful, growing up in such a large family!"

Wilf smiled easily. "It had its moments. You're from a small family?"

"I have just one sister. Can you tell me more of your mother's teachings?"

"I...uh...Well, I don't often speak of such things."

"I appreciate that." Kerensa smiled sweetly. "But I would also appreciate your making an exception for me—for my strictly scientific curiosity, of course."

Carefully Wilf regarded the young woman, trying to see past her dark glasses and into her soul. Where on earth, he thought, suddenly anxious again, was Clive? Surely it couldn't take him this long to drop Ann off at the pharmacy and then return—

"Of course," he finally responded, choosing his words carefully. "Mother was a teacher. I don't think she ever let an opportunity slip by for inserting her values into our souls. Now every one of us believes in telling the truth, even when it's inconvenient. Except for yours truly, we are unfailingly polite and do our best to be kind-hearted and not critical. And again except for yours truly, the ones who are married are faithful to their companions. And none of my siblings, so far as I know, has been sexually active before marriage."

"And you?"

"Are you serious? After Mom and her never-ending teaching? You have no idea how embarrassed I've been, admitting first to one person and then to another, that I'm a virgin! Even in high school—where I *didn't* talk about it—word got out and somebody made up a chant about me! I hated it!"

"That amazes me," Kerensa smiled." If I were you, I would proudly announce that I am virtuous, for it is a state of being I have come to cherish with all my heart!"

"Well," Wilf grumbled, "don't misunderstand. It doesn't bother me anymore that I've become what seems an anomaly in a vast sea of degradation and worldliness. The very things the world now espouses and proclaims sicken me with their banality and stupidity. At this stage in my life, I am quite happy to be my mother's son."

"I am pleased to hear that." Kerensa's look was serious. "But back to your family—your siblings. What you have just told me is astounding, Wilford, simply remarkable! Do you realize how amazingly rare their sexual fidelity actually is?"

"I've never thought of it that way." Reaching up, Wilf scratched his head. "Of course, I do understood how strange such values and standards seem outside Thatcher, Arizona. There, though—well, such was the power of Mother's convictions that I doubt any of us will ever seriously cross the line—any line she helped us establish."

"Absolutely amazing!"

"Actually, it isn't. A divorce has shattered one brother's family, and another brother has certainly tested the boundaries of Mother's—and his wife's—propriety. Yet my boundary-testing brother has waded through his mistakes and come back stronger than ever, and time has proven not only my divorced brother's innocence in the causes of his divorce but the tragic sadness of his former wife's duplicity and infidelity. Even better, he is now married to a woman who loves him as he has always deserved, he is reciprocating fully, and the rest of us are delighted with their happiness."

"I've watched it all, Kerensa, as well as the pain from all sorts of additional trials and difficulties in the lives of every one of them. None of us seems able to escape the world, so to speak, for we're very much like everyone else. Yet there seems to be a strength or staying power in Mother's beliefs and, except for myself, the family has been blessed by them."

"You have not been so blessed?"

Soberly Wilf shook his head. "Not really. At least I haven't thought so. What troubles me, I suppose, and troubles me deeply, is that in spite of my adherence to Mother's belief system, I also fit perfectly the description you gave a few moments ago of our wayward generation."

"What do you mean?"

"I mean that I am not a happy man! I am not at peace! These are emotions Mother led me to expect—at least if I did the things she taught me. Well, I've done as she asked, Kerensa, but instead of finding happiness and peace, I have remained fiddlefooted and tenuous, never really feeling a desire to commit myself to anything. For more than a decade, I've been wandering from one place to another, one school to another, one job to another. At thirty-four, I am mostly proficient in two languages, have made several deans' lists, and am fairly well read in a variety of disciplines. I also have all sorts of menial job skills that I do not care to ever market again. In other words, not only have I never graduated from college, but my life seems pointless because I remain absolutely unable to think of a career in which I wish to invest my life!

"But most troublesome of all—and why I am telling you all this I have no idea—is that all my failures seem to hinge on the very beliefs and expectations Mother ingrained so deeply within me. Therefore I, Wilford Abbott, ever-dutiful third son and fourth child of parents I continue to love dearly, do not know if I believe in a single thing that my mother's—and by association, my father's—lives embodied!"

Willing himself to stop, Wilf breathed deeply of the misty silence. The air smelled wonderfully clean, like on the ranch after a similar spring storm, and abruptly Wilf was homesick. With all his heart he longed to be back in Arizona with his family, or even anywhere instead of Cornwall, blabbing out his soul to an inquisitive woman who couldn't have cared less!

Where on earth, he wondered again, was that blasted Clive? Where, when he needed the man to hurry?

Of course, he thought gratefully, he hadn't told Kerensa Tansin everything, such as the fact that for two days he had thought himself in love with a schoolgirl who had now turned out to be—and it almost killed him to actually think this—a troubled spirit, a ghost! Or, and perhaps this was the most important issue of all, that his failure to be married hinged on the same beliefs and expectations that had brought to pass every other miserable failure in his life. Why? Because he had never yet met a woman with whom he had connected emotionally, which his mother had promised him a hundred times over would one day come to pass.

He hadn't, that is, unless he dared to count his more-than-strange experiences with the girl at the crossing—the same who was ten long years deceased and gone.

Chapter Sixteen

"Well, I see you two have met," Clive beamed past his wide, thick mustaches as he strode around the corner of the office, his navy wool stocking cap pulled tightly over his flowing gray hair. "Has he agreed then, Kerensa?"

"You two know each other?" Wilf questioned as he lunged to his feet, so surprised that he didn't immediately catch the meaning of Clive's question.

"Indubitably, we do!" Clive was still all smiles. "Our friendship with dear Kerensa developed last evening, Wilford, when Ann and I attempted most sincerely to retrieve you from *The Copley Arms.* Instead of you, however, we discovered this lovely young lady, who was herself in dire need of assistance. While Ann drove the trusty Passat back here alone, I had the great fortune of giving my services to our dear Kerensa."

"It sounds like you got along famously, all right." Wilf was feeling put out with Clive's involvement with the social anthropologist, though he had no idea why. "So, Clive, how did you get home?"

"Why," the elderly man's look was one of surprise, "I drove Kerensa, of course. In her rental."

"What? But you just said...I mean...Wait a minute! I seem to be missing something here. For some reason, Kerensa, I thought you were using the bu...I mean, coach. I distinctly heard you tell Petroc to purchase another ticket, just before you fired him!"

Kerensa laughed with astonishment. "You heard that? And I thought my hearing was good!"

"It probably is. So, why did you need Clive to drive you?"

Kerensa looked bewildered. "Because I'd given Petroc the sack and sent him packing, Wilford. The ticket I was speaking of was for you. Only I...I didn't see you again, and then I...got involved and missed the last coach. Thank heaven Clive came along to drive my car back here to Granite Henge. Otherwise I have no idea what I'd have done."

"Driven it back yourself, maybe?" Wilf questioned sarcastically, not even noticing Kerensa's discomfort.

"Are you serious? Wilford, I can't drive. I thought you knew that."

"Knew what?" Wilf was now shaking his head. "How could I have known that you can't drive?"

"How? By looking at me, I suppose." Kerensa was suddenly flustered. "Can't you see that I am blind?"

"You're *what*?" Wilf was absolutely astounded.

"She is blind, Wilford. Our dear Kerensa has lost her sight."

Wilf looked at Clive in bewilderment. "I...I know what being blind means, Clive. Are you trying to tell me that you knew it just by looking at her?" He was now speaking of Kerensa as though she were no longer there. "Or did she tell you when you went to the pub to find me?"

Clive grinned widely. "She didn't have to say anything, Wilford. I noted it straight away and immediately offered my services. You should have seen her blindness, too, my young friend. It surprises me that you did not."

"Well," Wilf admitted sheepishly, "I didn't."

"Lovely," Clive grinned. "Absolutely lovely. Kerensa's blind, and it's Wilford who cannot see."

"Actually," Kerensa finally volunteered, "we are discussing legal blindness, which is not quite the same as being totally sightless. Certain individuals experience the juvenile onset of

Hereditary Macular Dystrophy. That means they—we, I mean—can easily see light and darkness, though sunlight or even bright indoor lighting bothers our eyes terribly. We also see larger objects, such as people or homes or roadways, though without any of the details the rest of you take for granted. We read, but only Braille; we can't see pictures, and visually, I personally have no idea what any of you actually look like."

"Visually? Does that mean you have another way?"

Kerensa laughed. "Well, many sightless persons have a sense or feeling for how things look. I suppose you might say I am one of them. For instance, Clive, I see you as tall, properly straight like any good soldier, quite thin, silver hair that flows back and is a little long, and wonderfully handsome."

"Exactly," Clive beamed. "Brilliant! You have me to a 'T.' Especially the wonderfully handsome part!"

Kerensa laughed. "As for Ann, she is the perfect grandmother type—short, a little round, hair nowhere near as gray as yours because she is obviously much younger, and cut quite short because she doesn't like to waste time fussing with it—"

"Too short!" Clive interrupted with a teasing scowl. "The old girl's cut all the lovely curl off of it. And why, I might ask since we're on the subject, is it so obvious that she is much younger than me?"

"Because she sounds younger, Clive, and busier. Whereas you delight in taking the time for teasing and posing and posturing, Ann has little patience for such things, which she thinks are frivolous. While you are redundant and therefore free with your time, I now know that Ann is still working, still very much caught up in the societal burdens of day-to-day living."

"Well," Clive groused good-naturedly, "both of us very much resemble those remarks, and I believe you should know it."

"Thank you."

"What about young Wilford here? How do you suss him out?"

Kerensa laughed nervously. "Actually, Clive, Wilford is a little more difficult."

"Why?" Wilf asked pointedly. "Has someone told you about my baldness? If not, now you know, so don't let that bother you."

"He's a sensitive young thing, what?"

Kerensa nodded. "He seems to be. Very well, Wilford, I'd judge you at six feet or a little more in height, thin almost to the point of being gaunt, wiry build that hides a rather remarkable strength, and hair that is probably light brown but balding, most likely in the back."

"Here, here," Clive laughed, "I couldn't have done it better!"

"There's something else, too," Kerensa continued, her voice lower. "I don't know exactly how to describe this, Wilford, but in a way I sense that you are very—well, dangerous is the only word that comes to mind. I don't mean as a fighter, though poor Petroc might disagree with me. Rather it is something else—not sinister so much as deep and well-hidden—a power or force that others cannot for long oppose. In fact, I—but that's far more than enough for one reading of the tea leaves!"

"I'll say!" Wilf declared, feeling decidedly uncomfortable. "And all that comes of being blind? Mercy me!"

"How do you get around?" Clive quickly asked. "You don't use a cane, at least that I've seen."

The anthropologist shrugged. "I have one, Clive, but I absolutely detest using it. That's what Petroc was for. He was to drive the car, assist me in finding my way to new places and through new situations, and make me aware of what was transpiring around me. To be honest, though, I have become quite gifted in my mobility. Once I've been to a place, I can return to it by myself without difficulty!"

"Good for you!" the older man declared heartily. "Four remaining senses will always take over for the missing fifth, and then become extra sensitive. Happens all the time, you know. I saw it during the war."

"How do you manage your research? Besides reading Braille, I mean."

"Don't you mean besides asking so many personal questions?" Again Kerensa smiled. "That's another gift, Wilford.

When I'm at an archaeological site, if conditions are right and I am able to focus properly, then in my mind I am able to 'see' life as it was being lived by the ancients who once dwelt or fought or worshipped there. Or at least I believe that is what I am seeing."

"Is that sort of research accepted?" Clive asked.

"It seems to be—at least the way I do it."

"What sort of conditions are you referring to?"

"Oh, a great many little things, Wilford. I must be alone, as much as possible I must dress and act the part of the people I am studying, my mind must be free and clear of all other distractions—these sorts of things. When all the elements align themselves properly so I can 'see,' then I experience what the world seems to think of as success."

"Jolly good!" Clive was obviously impressed.

"Perhaps it is," Kerensa responded quietly, "but I assure you that such accolades are of no significance whatsoever, especially in light of my present task. In that, unfortunately, I am at a complete standstill, and now that I have no assistant, I have no idea how I will manage!"

"Ahh," Clive nodded, "so you haven't yet spoken of this to Wilford."

Suddenly embarrassed, Kerensa shook her head.

"Ahh," Wilf mimicked Clive with sudden understanding as he lunged to his feet, "so that's it! That's what you meant, Clive, when you first arrived! Well, finally this is making a little sense! The two of you are in cahoots, and I'm the intended victim! Or servant, or assistant, or whatever Petroc was going to be called. Well, *Dr. Tansin*, the answer is no! Flat and simple. *No!* Is that clear enough?

"Now, Clive, if you'll just get me down to Looe and the railroad station like you promised earlier, I'll be gone as the sun in winter! I have other places to go, things to do, people to meet—"

"Must I remind you that you owe me, Wilford?" Kerensa's smile was more sweet than ever. "Dearly?"

"Kerensa's right, you know." Clive now looked deadly serious. "After all, if you hadn't come along to put your boot to poor Petroc's wrist and other bodily parts—"

"Whoa! Hold up here! All I did was get back Ann's stolen purse and then defend myself from Orange-hair's miserable knife—twice, I might add! And I probably saved your bacon, too, Dr. Tansin! So, who owes whom?"

"You're absolutely right, Wilford," Kerensa beamed. "Therefore I shall pay you handsomely—five hundred pounds a day and all expenses!"

"Five hundred quid a day?" Clive gasped as his eyes widened. "My goodness, young lady! That's terribly—"

"Of course you're right, Clive; it should be more, much more! So, there'll also be a bonus at the end if I am successful—say, five thousand pounds?"

"Now that you mention it," Clive said as he playfully pushed Wilf to the side, "I'm an absolute expert at driving that new Mercedes automobile you've let."

"Very well, Clive, you're hired. But you told me last evening how you needed to help your sweet Ann. Now that you're to be with me day in and day out, what will you ever do about her?"

"Ann? Ann whom, might I ask? I know of no one named Ann. Just ask me!" Clive grinned mischievously. "Now, my dear, does that five hundred quid begin today, or are we to start in the morning?"

Abruptly Wilf laughed. Even though he was experiencing every warning signal his body and mind had ever developed, he determinedly forced them all to be still. There was no good way out of this, at least that he could see, and he certainly didn't want someone like Petroc trying to take advantage of the woman. Besides, he suddenly wondered, was Orange-hair really gone? Or had he and his idiot green-haired brother—

"All right, all right," he chuckled lightly. "I guess in a way this *is* my fault, so I'll stay. But I won't do it for money, Kerensa, and that's final! Not a dime—or whatever such a coin is called in this country. I'll give you one week, no more, and then I'm gone."

"Like the sun in winter," Kerensa smiled sweetly.

"Exactly." Wilf grinned malevolently. "Now one final question. Are you really staying here in Granite Henge, or was your presence here by the pool just part of yours and Clive's diabolical little plot?"

"I'm staying in the bungalow right over there," Kerensa pointed as she also rose to her feet. "I took the other side of the bungalow for Petroc, of course. But since he's no longer with us, Wilford, you're welcome to it." Now she smiled just as wickedly. "That way your snoring won't trouble poor Ann and Clive a moment longer!"

And with a squeal of laughter, the blind anthropologist somehow twisted out of Wilf's suddenly reaching hand.

Chapter Seventeen

"*T*his is a Mercedes?" In spite of the chill and closeness of the early morning fog, which was thicker than anything Wilf had yet seen, he was already enjoying himself. Though he didn't know Kerensa Tansin all that well, there had nevertheless developed between them a certain closeness that allowed, if nothing else, enough familiarity to tease. In his life, Wilf had felt such freedom with few women other than his sisters, and he was delighted to be experiencing it now. "This vehicle looks more like an egg that's been squashed on both ends—a dark green egg, at that!"

Kerensa laughed lightly. "Yes, that does quite accurately describe it. But the emblem on the boot is definitely Mercedes and so was the cost of a month's rental. I feel confident, therefore, of its authenticity."

"And the steering wheel's on the wrong side, too! Good grief, lady! Next you'll probably be telling me I have to drive on the wrong side of the road!"

"No, I'd rather you didn't," Kerensa smiled. "Just stay on the left side, which of course is the right side."

"That makes perfect sense!"

"It would if you'd reason it through. Are all Americans so cantankerous and obstinate?"

"Probably not. My sister Julie says those are my particular gifts." Wilf held the left- hand door open for his passenger, then went around to the right and settled behind the wheel. "Did I happen to mention that I'm severely dyslexic? Never have been able to tell left from right."

"How very tragic!" Kerensa sympathized.

"I mean it! Just look at my boots! The toes are almost always pointed off in the wrong direction."

"In spite of my blindness I am looking," the social anthropologist replied sweetly, "and they look perfectly aligned to me. A little scuffed and in need of a polish, perhaps—"

"Hey, that's enough from the cheap seat!"

"I daresay. But I shouldn't worry much about your dyslexia if I were you. In this fog it won't matter, for no one will be driving on the proper side of the road."

"That's comforting!"

"Yes, isn't it. Are we ready to begin?"

Wilf grinned. "Yeah, if I can just find the ignition—ouch! Dog-gone door shouldn't be here on my right side! Now I've lost half the skin off my favorite knuckle! All right, the engine's running, and I think I may have this shifter figured out. So, where are we going?"

"Not far from here, actually. With the fog I thought it best to start close—at the Talland Church."

"A church?" Wilf was suddenly concerned about visiting the Talland Church, though he intended to act innocent before Kerensa Tansin. Nevertheless, the body of Morwenna Miller had been buried at the Talland Church in an unmarked grave, according to Jeanette Fellick, either because she was a suicide or because the graveyard was too full! This was why both Jeanette and Ann thought Morwenna's ghost was so miserable. She was still waiting for a final resting place.

Yesterday he'd completely dismissed the idea of finding and then taking a look around the old church, but now that he would be there—

"Wilford, did you hear me?"

"Yeah," he responded lamely, "Talland Church. Is that on the hill up from Polperro?"

"Actually, no. That is Talland Hill, of course, but the church is on around to the northeast of Talland Bay. That is over the hill from Polperro, or around Downend Point, depending on how one chooses to travel."

"Talland Bay? That's right." Truthfully, Wilf's exhausted mind was having trouble remembering. He'd had no idea jet-lag could be so pervasive. "A couple of days ago, I took the coastal path out of Polperro as far eastward as the War Memorial above Downend Point before I turned off. Had I continued, I believe the path would have led me on around to Talland Bay."

"Yes, and then on to Portnadler Bay and from there into Looe—a brisk trek of about five miles. Very good. Now, Talland Church is set back to the northeast from Talland Bay, at the top of the bluff. That means you won't be driving toward Polperro at all. When you pull out of our carpark, therefore, turn right and then almost immediately turn right again. That road will be quite narrow, so you must drive rather slowly—"

"Yes, ma'am! Yes, ma'am! Three bags full!"

"What? Oh, yes, the nursery rhyme—oh, dear Wilford, do forgive me! I must sound positively dictatorial. But I forget you are not one of my immature assistants."

"Well," Wilf grinned as he peered into the fog while driving the car gingerly forward, "I may be more immature than I look, but I still don't like being bossed around. As a matter of fact, I might—hey, you forgot to tell me there was a stop sign here!"

"Goodness, yes! This is the main route from Looe to Polperro. Please continue straight on across it, kind sir."

Carefully Wilf crossed the highway and continued southward into the fog. Though it was fully light, he could see little enough of the countryside, just the occasional looming shape of a house or large tree set close to the narrow road. It, meanwhile, wound and turned remarkably. Yet somehow Kerensa always sensed where they were and was quick with directions that would lead them to the old church.

"How do you do that?" he asked at one point when she actually had to stop him and have him reverse.

"I study maps."

"In Braille?"

Kerensa laughed. "As you would put it, not hardly. I have students read them to me, or rather I have them describe the routes precisely that I wish to take. It is, therefore, a simple matter of memory."

"Simple? I don't think so, Kerensa. For a fact, I don't think there's anything simple about you!"

"Why, my dear Wilford, that sounded very much like another compliment! Your second in my behalf, I do believe."

"Good." Wilf was straining to see out the window. "Wait a minute! There's something big up ahead. High? Square top?"

"Yes, that's the church tower or steeple. You've done it, Wilford; you've brought us here without difficulty! Now, immediately to your left is a small carpark—"

"I'll say its small," Wilf responded as he turned into a space off the road that was barely large enough for two cars—British cars, that is.

"Good. Now, my dear assistant, I may be an hour or so, and I must remain absolutely alone! Do you understand?"

"No, not really. But I'll leave you alone, if that's what you are saying."

"It is, but you must also protect me from others. Look around inside the church if you wish, and take a walk through the cemetery. You'll find both very old, very quaint. You will especially enjoy seeing the old stocks."

"Stocks? You mean where they lock peoples' heads into holes between two boards?"

"Well done, Wilford! In Talland Church's case, the stocks held both the heads and wrists of two people, most of whom were no doubt nosey women who had been charged with gossiping."

"Yeah," Wilf grinned, "by the ones they had been gossiping about, I wonder?"

Kerensa laughed. "No doubt! Now remember, I'll be somewhere on the bluff beyond the church. If others come to visit, please ask them to stay in the churchyard proper. That is where they'll find the graves, you know. Tell them I am a scientist, conducting an important experiment—"

"Is that the truth?"

Kerensa smiled. "I'd not ask you to lie."

"No, I suppose you wouldn't. And you won't tell me what it is you're after?"

Kerensa shook her head. "As I explained last evening when you asked the same question, Wilford, I cannot. However, perhaps one day—"

"Well," Wilf chuckled, "you can't blame a guy for persevering. Can you get where you're going okay? I mean, the fog's pretty thick—"

"Wilford," Kerensa giggled, "to me, the fog is always thick!"

"Oh, yeah." Feeling foolish, Wilf climbed out of the car and retrieved Kerensa's pack from the trunk. "Now, let me get this straight. In England, the trunk is called the boot?"

"Yes, and your hood is our bonnet. Wilford, I must be—"

"But the tires are still tires?"

Again the social anthropologist giggled. "Why do I have the feeling that you wish me to stay?"

"Because it's true. I wish you'd at least let me go with you. Your going off alone makes me nervous as an earthworm at a convention of hungry robins!"

"Quaint, Wilford. Very quaint. But I promise you, I'll be fine. Please don't forget that I must be left alone!"

"Yes, my dear Kerensa," Wilf teased, using one of hers and the Paynes' favorite expressions which, now that he'd heard it coming out of his own mouth, sounded good. In silence, he then watched as Kerensa entered the churchyard and quickly vanished into the thick fog, her movements sure and steady. Well, he thought as he climbed back into the Mercedes to read a brochure on the old church he'd pulled out of the boot with her backpack, maybe she was blind and could tell without difficulty where she was going in such pea soup. That, he'd willingly admit. Still, such a gift couldn't change the fact that there was something about all this that was wrong! What it might be, he didn't know. But *something* inside him was jangling a nagging warning.

If only he hadn't promised to leave her alone....

There's an aspect of human behavior that some have called the principle of least interest. As Wilf was beginning to figure out, this principle means that in any relationship—marriage, business, or whatever—the one with the least interest controls the situation. That's because he or she is less concerned about consequences and so feels greater freedom to do things or make decisions that can harm or even destroy the relationship. In other words, they simply care more for themselves than they do the one being hurt.

Whole societies, obviously, are affected by this same principle. Consider, for instance, the lengths special interest groups go to in order to achieve their "special interests." How many are hurt by such campaigns? Or too many of our politicians, who care more for power and prestige than they do the people. Or—and this should be most obvious of all—those who believe that laws were made for everyone but them. This is the huge but shadowy force for chaos and destruction we call criminal or terrorist, but which Wilf was starting to see must include any or all of us who ignore any law or rule that might bring devastation, trauma or heartache into the life of another....

Chapter Eighteen

With a start, Wilf sat up, blinking his eyes rapidly. Without intending to, he'd fallen asleep while reading about the old church.

"Oh, no!" he grimaced as he glanced at his watch, "Kerensa's been gone an hour! For crying out loud, Wilford Abbott! Can't you do *anything* right?"

Lunging from the Mercedes, he ran into and through the churchyard, dodging the ancient headstones as they loomed out of the fog, ducking under the wagon porch, and continuing to where the crowded graveyard dropped steeply down the hill. So far as he could tell, however, he was utterly alone with the church and the weathered old monuments. There was no sign that anyone had recently come up the steep trail, and he knew someone coming from his direction would have awakened him. Which meant, he thought with relief, that Dr. Tansin was still alone on the bluff and doing her thing!

A slight breeze stirred the heavy fog, and above him through the trees and fog, the square, flat-topped stone steeple suddenly loomed. Built a short distance apart from the church, it was, he guessed, between fifty and sixty feet high and perhaps twenty to twenty-five feet wide at the base. There were thin, arched windows in what must be the top story or floor, and there was also a narrow door midway down, though it opened onto no landing that he could discern. It was the flat top of the old steeple, however, that interested Wilf the most. Rather than rising to a point, the top was buttressed like an ancient castle. Now why, he wondered, would a bunch of old clerics build themselves a church tower like that? Might it have been that they, too, needed a place for defense? And might it also be why they separated the tower from the church—so the place of worship wouldn't be desecrated by battle and killing?

Grinning at the thought, Wilf retraced his steps to the car, where he removed the key and locked the door. Then he set out to explore, doing his best to keep from his mind both the unsettling presence of Kerensa Tansin, as well as the fact that somewhere nearby lay the unclaimed body of a troubled schoolgirl called Morwenna Miller.

Turning back through the gate, Wilf moved through the long grass and past the first of the gravesites. He could now see that someone had recently cut the grass on the path, for it was shorter than the lush growth around it. Still it was deep, and with the fog hampering his view, Wilf found the going more difficult than he had expected. It was also much slower, for he could hardly restrain himself from trying to read the names on the old monuments he was passing.

And some of them were very old! Large granite and iron crosses, some of them Celtic surrounded by ornate circles, were so pitted with age, so covered with moss and lichen, that no sign of names or dates even remained. Others, obviously more recent, were engraven slabs of slate cut perhaps two inches thick by two feet wide by up to four feet in height, their tops cut in all sorts of rounded, scrolled, or other ornamented shapes. A good many of these were at least partially readable, such as one for a William Morthcott, Builder. Yet birth and death dates, engraven in much smaller script, were so obscured by weathering that Wilf could see none older than the mid 1700s.

Of course, he wasn't exactly going from grave to grave looking, either. As the fog shifted and drifted in and out with the now-fitful breeze, hiding and then revealing the ancient church and its hilly graveyard, Wilf found himself growing more and more worried. The quiet of the place was intense, too intense, it seemed to him. Besides, the fog was taking away his horizons, causing him to feel almost as if the eerie churchyard had become somehow isolated from the rest of the world.

As he approached the church itself, Wilf discovered that the path or ancient roadway was lined with gravestones, just as David Fellick had said, and that the tower and church proper had been connected by what Kerensa had called a wagon-porch, obviously providing parishioners a little shelter for loading and unloading from horse-drawn carts during inclement weather.

Inside the church, which to his surprise he found open but empty, Wilf saw that the structure was double-roofed, with a row of supporting arches running along the center. The altar was back-lit by a three-paned stained-glass window, the wooden pews boasted ornately carved bench ends, and the baptistry, just inside the door, contained an ornately carved stone bowl from which parishioners were obviously sprinkled. There was also a stone monument near the entry, secured to the wall, memorializing one Robert Mark, a fisherman and popular local smuggler who had been slain by the Crown's 'Preventive Men' a couple of hundred years before.

So Kerensa had been right about that, too, he thought with a grin. At one time, smuggling had been very important along the Cornish coast, with dark-of-night comings and goings, hidden caves, and secret ways and doings that now were lost forever. And with Robert Mark, no doubt the old church was memorializing one of its faithful own.

As he strolled about, Wilf recalled reading that the church was built on the site of an earlier Celtic church established by Irish Christian missionaries during the fourth or fifth century. Though dedicated to Saint Tallanus, the brochure had pointed out that such a person may never even have existed. Saint was a later addition to the original Cornish name of Tal Lan, which meant 'the holy place' *(lan)* on 'the brow of the hill' *(tal)*.

He also found an inscription written in old Cornish, which read *Bengys yu nep a-gar Dew dres pup tra us y'n bys.* Beneath it, a translation declared, 'Blessed is the person who loves God before everything else.'

"Well," he muttered with a wry grin as he moved on, "there you go, Robert Mark. If you'd stayed away from smuggling to better love the Lord, you might not have been dead for quite so long a time!"

Outside again, Wilf discovered, almost hidden under the porch, the place where Kerensa's 'stocks' had been, or at least so said a small sign. The stocks were gone, however, and only some slight impressions on a walled shelf indicated they had ever been there at all.

Wilf was still considering the missing stocks as he tried the heavy wooden doors of the tower, found them locked tightly, and so climbed around behind the ancient tower and into the upper graveyard, passing such an array of lichen-covered crosses, gravestones, and even boxed stone sepluchers, as to leave him feeling awed by the sense of both history and human mortality. Ahead of him the hill seemed to brow, and beyond it the fog had thinned enough to reveal a clump of tall coastal pines—a sight Wilf found breathtakingly beautiful.

Drawn forward, he continued to climb until he reached the hill's brow. There a small set of stairs led down the other side, past large bushes of gorse and into a grassy pasture. This in turn sloped down toward the giant, shrouded pines and then down from there into the fog's gray oblivion. Yet the ocean was hidden somewhere below, Wilf knew, for he could hear the waves crashing in off the English Channel, spending their churning and frothing rebellion against the rocky bastion of hard granite cliffs.

Turning at a slight sound that was much closer, Wilf saw, not Kerensa Tansin as he had hoped, but two horses munching grass nearby—saw them and then did not, for the fog shifted again and drew both animals back into its gray obscurity. Yet now he noticed, not thirty feet away but well within the pasture, two solitary graves that had been covered with small stones, one obviously more recently than the other. Otherwise unmarked, Wilf nevertheless knew as he walked slowly forward, his heart pounding wildly, that he had found the final, lonely resting place of the girl at the crossing—the girl with the Cornish name of Morwenna Miller.

For some time Wilf sat near the lonely grave, his mind awash with solemnities. What was it that had brought him to Cornwall? The suggestion of some American girl whose name he didn't even recall? Yes. But somehow it seemed that there must have been more, some ill-defined something that had not only brought him to this haunted land of ghosts and legends but had placed him in the very position where he could see one for himself. More significantly, he had been brought to a place where others could see her also, lest he begin to doubt.

Sighing deeply, Wilf thought about that. For a fact, over the years he himself had become a doubter. As a child and then young man, he had believed fervently. But then things had happened—hard and painful things—and the notion of a kind and loving God implanted in his heart by his mother had faded into doubt.

Yet now, because of what he and the Paynes had seen, he could no longer ignore his family's belief in life after death. Yes, he'd always thought of Missy and his parents as being *somewhere*, though in a rather nebulous sort of way. Now it had all become real, and in part he had Clive and Ann to thank for it. Still, to him alone had been given the communication, the glorious sense that Morwenna Miller had been waiting forever for him to come. Of course he had no earthly idea why he should have received such an impression, but still he'd felt the power of it, and so he knew!

For some reason, though, Wilf was suddenly feeling drained of emotion, utterly exhausted. Were things never going to stop being hard? Was he never going to experience a little joy, a little peace? First he'd given his heart to a ghost, and now a famous social anthropologist was turning out to be amazingly attractive! It was just too much! Morwenna Miller, the girl for whom his mother's promised sign had been given, was lying in an unmarked grave in a horse pasture overlooking Talland Bay in Cornwall of the British Isles! And despite the fact that Kerensa Tansin was so incredibly lovely in every imaginable way, he couldn't stop himself from thinking about Morwenna Miller.

Angrily, Wilf shook his head. But he had not been able to find her—not even a trace—and so, finally, he was done with it! Whatever the meaning of her appearances, whatever the message in her communications, Morwenna Miller was now part of his past, not his future. He, Wilford Abbott, was moving on!

As proof, he thought with a wry grin, he was now spending time with Kerensa Tansin, a sweet and lovely woman who could set any man's heart to fluttering, certainly including his own if he would give it half a chance. As a matter of fact Wilf liked her—liked her a great deal—and it had been that which had persuaded him to stay. After all, who wouldn't want to spend a week in the company of so beautiful and accomplished a woman? The fact that she was blind and that he might actually be of service to her had been an added incentive. But mainly, Wilf admitted candidly, he simply enjoyed being near her!

Speaking of which, he thought as he rose stiffly to his feet, it was time to track her down. She had asked only for an hour, perhaps a little more. Now he felt justified in going after her, in making certain that all was well. The dilemma, of course, was that he hadn't the least notion of where to look!

The bluff? Yes, so she had said. But where? Which bluff? Or rather, which part of the bluff that extended along every part of the Cornish coast he had managed to see, might she be occupying to do her work? Where in the world had Kerensa Tansin gone? Where should he begin—

The scream, when he heard it, was distant, and for a fraction of a second he wasn't sure he had heard it at all. But then it came again, faint but long and tremulous, and he knew! Kerensa was in trouble! Somewhere back in the direction of the old church—

Heedlessly plunging up the steps at the top of the bluff and into the ancient graveyard, Wilf ran and slid down the winding path through the gravestones. He should start with the car, he was thinking frantically. If she was not there, then he would search the church before working his way back up and onto the bluff again. Hopefully, by then the fog would have lifted, at least a little, and he would stand a better chance.

Wilf didn't know what made him glance over his shoulder, yet he did—and was dumbfounded to see, standing near the upper steps he had just crossed over, the girl from the crossing! She was not moving but was gazing ahead of him, in the direction he was going, and the thought came unbidden that she might be signaling someone—

With a strangled cry Wilf slowed himself, turned, and started through the moisture- slick grass toward her, intent on getting to her before she could disappear again! This wasn't possible, of course! He couldn't be seeing Morwenna Miller's spirit! Not again! Yet if he wasn't, then who or what—

"Morwenna!" he shrieked in desperation, finally knowing that the apparition he had been seeing wasn't mortal. *"Morwenna Miller!* I know it's you! It has to be you! Turn around, please, and talk to me—"

A sudden, blinding pain smashed into the back of Wilf's head, and an instant later he found himself face down in the long, wet grass. With a lunge he sprang for his feet, determined to confront who or what had hit him. Only the slick leather soles of his boots betrayed him, he lost his balance, and as a searing pain slashed his side he went down again, spinning out of control in a frightening tumble into the ancient gravestones.

"Blimey, Pet!" Wilf heard dimly as he lay in a heap, unable to move. "It's the Yank we've popped! Joe Bloggs himself!"

"I know who he is, you stupid nit!" This was a different voice, one that sounded far too familiar. Petroc Penryn! The young man who continually persisted in trying to kill him! The one who—

"What do you think I cut him for?"

"But...Alistair said for us to leave him be if he showed up! To stay clear of him!"

"Shut your gab, you yob! Alistair ain't been done by this bloke the way we have! Twice for me! The Yank's had it coming, he has!"

"Is he dead, then? Have you killed him, Pet?"

"Naw, he twisted, somehow, so he ain't dead. He's hurting, though! Just look at all the blood. Ha! Finally me blade gave the arrogant bloke a little of what he's been asking for! I'd do more to him, too, and gladly! Only, Alistair's due along any minute—"

Unable to move, or even to groan, Wilf lay with his face against a gravestone. He knew he'd been hurt, probably badly. He also knew it was Petroc who had done it—he and his younger brother, Neville. The trouble was, Wilf couldn't do anything about it. He couldn't even find Kerensa—

"We going to leave him where he is, then?"

"Leave him here for somebody to find? You nit! Are you daft? Grab those ugly boots while I get his shoulders, and we'll put him in the old smugglers' hole! Since there ain't no way out, that'll be the end of him, sure! Too bad, too. I wouldn't of minded doing a bit more cutting!"

With horrid oaths, the two brothers grabbed Wilf to move him, and the pain that instantly followed was so severe that Wilf's head swirled wildly, and he knew he was blacking out. Yet in the few seconds before it happened—and this was no surprise—he saw Morwenna Miller's ghost standing as before, her eyes now boring into his but sending forth no communication whatsoever!

Wilf tried to shout, couldn't, and in the next instant he felt himself being heaved and slid over rough stone. Then he was falling—for a long time he seemed to be falling; darkness was everywhere, and the last thing he remembered was the terrible pain that came when he hit bottom.

Then, thankfully, he could feel no more.

Chapter Nineteen

*W*ilf had no idea how long he had been unconscious. He wasn't even certain when his senses returned. Everything was too dark, too painful, and nothing changed when he moved or opened his eyes. Still, at some point he found himself sitting up rather than otherwise, and he was also conscious, finally, that beneath him was a bed of sand. There was a distant roaring in his ears, and after a time he realized he was listening to waves crashing one after another against some rocky shore.

Thus, slowly and almost imperceptibly, reason returned, and with it Wilf's memory of what had happened. Somehow, the two brothers had managed to club him over the head. Petroc had also got his knife into him—

Instantly concerned, Wilf began a careful self-examination to determine the extent of his injuries and to see whether or not, now that he knew he was alive, he was likely to remain that way. The examination was difficult in the inky blackness, not only because his entire body was so sore, but because he could not seem to maintain his equilibrium. Did Kerensa have a balance problem, he found himself wondering? Or other blind people? Or was it happening to him not because of the darkness but because he had taken such a brutal blow to his head?

And that made Wilf wonder, suddenly, if he might also be blind. Was the darkness, therefore, his own and not part of wherever he might presently be? The thought stunned him and became even more troubling when he realized there was no way he could be sure. No way, that is, unless he could find a way out of—of wherever this place was.

On the back of his head, beneath a great deal of matted blood, was a wide gash and some definite swelling. There was another gash across the side of his forehead, a gash that was still bleeding, for beneath it he could feel the blood's warm stickiness. His left arm and shoulder hurt intensely with every movement he made, but when he could discover no open wounds, he was left to surmise that it had been on that part of his body he had landed. A little better news was that despite the pain he could still move—a probable indication of no broken bones.

There was a long gash down his side and part way across his abdomen—Petroc's knife, no doubt. While painful, it wasn't deep, and Wilf counted himself fortunate that he had been wearing his loose jacket at the time of the attack. It was when he attempted to stand, however, that he discovered what he thought of as his most severe injury. His left ankle was so painful he couldn't put weight on it, and with the swelling he had no way of discerning a possible break.

"All right," he muttered, "I can stand but I can't walk, and even if I could, I can't keep my balance. Conclusion? Crawl. Problems with crawling? Unbearable pain in my arm and shoulder, and I have no earthly idea in what direction I should crawl! Second conclusion? Do it anyway, Wilf Abbott, or at least slither, because you won't get out of here by staying where you are!"

Get out? In wonder, Wilf realized that was correct. He was in a cave of some sort, or a huge underground room, from which he had to get out. Not only could he now recall being pushed over an old sepulcher wall and then falling into darkness, but in talking to himself moments before, he had heard a definite echo. He had been pushed into a large, sandy-floored cavern. Now he remembered his attackers calling it a smugglers' hole, no doubt one of the myriad coastal caves Kerensa had mentioned that first day at the pub. Now all he had to do was find the way those old boys had used to get in and out!

Which, he realized after the first few inches, was going to be tough! It ended up that he had to slither, and even then he was aware of the excruciating pain which brought merciful unconsciousness to him at least twice. On another occasion, he pulled his watch up to check the time, only to remember as he was again succumbing to the pain from his shoulder that he had purchased a cheap watch before leaving Arizona, disdaining the more expensive models with luminescent hands and face.

It seemed to take forever before the sand became moist, and Wilf knew he had come to the sea. The problem, though, was that at some previous time there must have been a cave-in, for though the waves and rising tides could seep in, wetting the sand, he could find no opening through which he might slither out. For a few moments, he tried digging into the sand, but that proved futile when he ran into solid rock less than a foot down—solid rock that was flooded with sea water. He also tried pulling loose rocks aside to create a hole a little higher up, but he could not move enough of them to make a difference.

Meanwhile, he had another thought. Kerensa Tansin! Rather than himself, it had to have been her the brothers were after. Hadn't he heard her screaming, at least twice? Surely that meant they had her! Only, how could they have known Kerensa would be visiting the old Talland Church—

Petroc! Even though he'd been employed less than a day, Kerensa as much as admitted showing him her schedule—or at least the places she intended to visit. She'd even entrusted him with her purse and her money, the keys to her rental, and—

"Oh, glory!" Wilf muttered. "That's it! They're after her money! In a way she's been flaunting it worse than she did her body, and that's bound to attract attention. So maybe it's the Mercedes and whatever cash and travelers cheques she has on her. And, somehow Petroc'll have made a duplicate key to her bungalow, too, the slimy toad! That'll give them a pretty good haul if they can sneak into Granite Henge and get away with it—"

"Wait a minute! Wilf Abbott, you ninny, why don't you use your head for something useful? Both those boys spoke of someone else while you were lying there groaning, someone with a name that seemed sort of familiar—that's it! Alistair MacLean, the novelist! *When Eight Bells Toll!* One of my favorite books. Of course it wasn't that Alistair they were talking about. He's been dead some time, now. But it was definitely someone named Alistair. And since Neville was afraid of him, Alistair whomever-he-is, has to be the big cheese in this company!

"That means they're holding Kerensa for ransom! Which means she's more than likely still alive—"

Abruptly Wilf's heart sank. "Unless the ransom's already been paid," he breathed in despair, "or they've killed her anyway but are carrying on as though she's alive. That's sometimes done—oh, no! Petroc's bound to be the one guarding her, and I never saw anyone filled with such a fever for a woman!"

In anguish, Wilf turned and crawled and slithered forward, forcing himself on until he had reached a rough stone wall. He couldn't tell if it had been cut by man or nature, but in a frenzy he felt his way along it, trying to discern something—anything —that might indicate a place of escape. He had to get to her! Somehow he had to get out of this hole so he could help Kerensa.

After a time the sand ended, and Wilf became aware that the floor was sloping upward, at least a little. Did that mean water came all the way to there, at least when the tide was in, carrying the sand with it? Or might sand have been deposited in the cave only during the worst of winter storms? Or before the cave-in at the mouth? Of course he had no way of knowing, but soon he came to the narrow rear of the cave, felt his way across it, and started on his belly and knees back down the other side, still finding no indication that there might have once been an opening other than the caved-in mouth.

After what seemed an eternity, he was back at the moist sand—whether the tide was coming in or going out he had no way of knowing—and Wilf knew he had failed. As Petroc and Neville had said, there was no way out! Even standing occasionally on one foot and reaching high as he could, he had found nothing! He was utterly and completely entombed and would never in this life get to Kerensa's aid—

"Wilford," a voice suddenly asked in his mind, "have you inquired of the Lord?"

Surprised at the vividness of the old memory, Wilf found himself wondering what had brought it to his mind. It was strange, he thought, that it should come now.Ten years before, only days before her death, his mother had asked him that question regarding an issue he had been struggling with: "Wilford, have you inquired of the Lord?" Not only had her question infuriated him, for of course he had not so inquired, but it had led to an estrangement between the two of them that he had not had time to resolve, not before she and his father had taken that fatal drive.

"Mother," he groaned in despair, for some reason again speaking audibly, "will the memories of your nagging *never* go away?"

"Why do you think it nagging," she continued softly, still echoing the old conversation Wilf remembered so distinctly, "when your brothers and sisters look on it as instructive?"

"Because I don't believe in that stuff!" Wilf shouted now as he had shouted then. "Besides, Mom, it isn't like I'm evil. I'm moral, just the way you taught me! I'm always trying to do good things for people, everywhere I go. Right now I'm even trying to help a blind woman—or at least I was until...anyway, Mom, I even talk to the Lord now and then—when I'm off and alone and no one is around to bother me."

"And what does he tell you, Wilford?"

No longer able to tell if he was remembering something from his past or hearing something from his present or for that matter even caring, Wilf continued to respond. "That isn't how it works for me, Mom, and you know it! When I pray, I do all the talking while the Lord does all the keeping silent. Those are his rules, by the way, not mine. If he's ever told me one single thing, I'd like to know of it."

"Very well, dear, I'm pleased you are praying. But remember, when you really need the Lord, you must exercise faith enough to be specific. Only then can he respond in specific ways. Think of the scripture, Wilford, and follow it: *Ask, and ye shall receive, Seek, and ye shall find, Knock, and it shall be opened unto you.*"

Shaking his head, Wilf tried to clear away the cobwebs of the old memory. But still it lingered, forcing him to recall how his mother had been—ever and always teaching, counseling, encouraging, cajoling, no matter whether or not he'd wanted any part of it! Which, after Missy's awful death, he had not! Not in any way—

"Wilford, she needs you!"

Startled, Wilf looked around into the darkness. It was her again, his mother's voice intruding into his mind. Only, he had no memory of her ever making such a statement—

"Ask, my dear son, and ye shall receive."

With a groan, Wilf covered his face with his hands. "Mom, I can't do it! You know that! God will never hear me—"

"Seek, Wilford, and ye shall find."

Now sobbing both in fear and frustration, but out of old habit, Wilf closed his eyes. Of course, in the darkness of the cave it made no difference, but—"Dear God," he began awkwardly. Then, again remembering, he started over. "Father in Heaven, you know why I don't talk to you. It...it isn't that I don't believe, though maybe now that's also true. It's just that, well, I can't! Not after what I...what happened! You know that; you know everything! So why did it have to happen...to me...to Missy? You could have stopped it, Father! It wouldn't even have been hard! But you didn't! And now I...I—"

"Knock, and it shall be opened unto you!"

Drawing a deep breath and swiping at his eyes with the ragged right sleeve of his jacket, Wilf pushed on. "All right, Mom, I hear you! Dear Father in Heaven, Mom...Mother, says...no, used to say...that you couldn't help me if I wasn't specific. All right, here's specific. Kerensa Tansin—she's a woman I met here in Cornwall, a good woman, I think, is in trouble! She's blind—I know you know all this, but I don't know how else to be specific! I think Kerensa's been kidnapped and is in serious danger! I'm not asking for me but for her, but if you could just show me how to get out of this cave, I...I'll do everything I can to help her. After that it doesn't matter so much, only someday, somewhere, I'd like to feel a little peace—"

Closing his prayer, Wilf opened his eyes and looked around. Nothing! The inky darkness was the same, the muted roar of the crashing waves continued without let-up—well, it was exactly what he had expected. With nothing more than a sigh of disappointment, for there *had* for a change been a tiny bit of hope, he rolled to his belly to start again—and realized he was lying on top of a stick of some sort. Squirming so he could pull it free of the sand, he was surprised to find it was a walking stick, ornately carved and probably quite old. Someone long ago, most likely one of Cornwall's inveterate and unrepentant smugglers, had left it behind.

Quickly Wilf pulled himself to his feet, balancing himself with the stick. This was better, he thought, a great deal better. Now he could not only walk, but he could poke and prod far up the walls, perhaps even to the roof of the cave. Maybe that was why he hadn't found an opening. Maybe it was high up, far out of reach of people like himself who had stumbled into the cave. Maybe the smugglers had made it high, to hide it from the Crown's "preventive men" such as those who had slain old Robert Mark, officers who would surely have been searching—

"Thank you for the stick, Father," he breathed, remembering another lesson from his mother. "Now, please help me use it to get out—"

Looking upward, Wilf was surprised that he could see a little of the shape of the cave. Turning toward where it lifted and narrowed at the rear, he was then dumbfounded to see, standing high up but looking down at him, the girl at the crossing—Morwenna Miller. Again everything about her was the same, including the communication! There was flowing from her to him the most amazing feeling of love, of complete acceptance. Yet, his struggling mind thought for a split second, there seemed also to be a difference.

Blinking to make certain this was real, and preparing to call her name, Wilf was just as astounded to find himself once again alone. There was no one with him in the cave, no one standing on what looked for all the world like small, narrow steps cut high into the rock.

"Thank you again," he breathed heavenward, this time with a slight smile, and moments later he had found the hand and footholds leading to the stairs and was painfully inching his way up, feeling his way with the stick and going carefully, much as the blind Kerensa would have done if she had been there beside him. And watching carefully, as he climbed, for the way Morwenna Miller had taken to elude him once again.

Chapter Twenty

"Well, Dr. Ren, how's these for holiday digs? Suit your high and fancy airs, do they?" Petroc laughed harshly, his younger brother Neville instantly joining in.

"Oiaye, Dr. Ren! Bet you never thought you'd suss out a flat like this one. You're the one for digging out antiquities and such. An old digs like this ought to fancy you just fine!"

"Shut up, Neville, you nit! It ain't no wonder the old lady's always called you them awful names. You're a nit for sure! It ain't no wonder she's made you sleep out in them old mews, either! With the spiders and bugs and all them rats and mice what live in stables, you fit in just right!"

"Petroc, that ain't true!" Neville looked as though his heart had been crushed. "Mum's loved me good! You know it's so! Didn't she give me all them rats and mice for my friends? And ain't it so that none of them's ever bit me, while you've been bit time and again?"

"I told you to shut your gob, Nev! If you can't suss out why, then I'll say it's because the lady on the floor there ain't like you! She's a smart one like me, she is, a famous scientist, and can suss out all sorts of things just by listening to you natter on. So shut up, I say! Put a sock in it!"

Kerensa Tansin, her head still pounding from where the two brothers had clubbed her only moments after she had left Wilford and the car, found herself blinking her eyes against the pain. Miraculously, her dark glasses had remained in place, though she could tell by the tightness of her cap that it must have been knocked off and then replaced on her head. Neville had even carried her pack up to the room, for she had seen him do it after her senses had returned, and even now she could see where he had dropped it in the far corner.

Of course she had been unconscious for some time, she knew, and now her throbbing back and legs were finally going numb from her unnatural position, giving her a measure of relief from the pain in them.

While difficult to focus her attention, still she listened to the heavy breathing of the Penryn brothers. She wasn't afraid of either of them, not really. Oh, she feared what Petroc was constantly threatening to do with her—no, that wasn't right. Actually the thought of it made her physically ill, which was not the same as fear. As a matter of fact, she didn't even fear dying and had often thought what a wonderful relief it might be. What she feared, therefore, was merely the unknown, the what-ifs she was now running through her mind.

The main thought, of course, had to do with Wilford Abbott. What if these two ignorant young men had actually killed him? They'd been bragging ever since she had regained consciousness that they'd "done him good," whatever that meant. But they'd revealed no details save that there had been a lot of blood, so Kerensa had no idea what had actually happened. If he were dead, though, then as far as she was concerned, her own life might as well end, too. After all, it was she who had persuaded him to stay, she who had enticed him into being her driver and assistant. And all the while she had known that, with one simple decision, there would have been no need at all for his help!

She could not bear such guilt! Especially not when—

And what of Wilford's sweet friends, the Paynes? Now Kerensa was intentionally refocusing her mind, willing it to leave the past to itself. Had Clive and Ann also become involved in this mess? There had been nothing to indicate that such was the case, but knowing Petroc as she was coming to know him, anything dastardly was possible.

Finally there was the man called Alistair, in large measure an unknown quantity who was giving the two brothers constant instructions via a cell phone kept a floor or two below. Still, from one-sided bits of conversation, she knew it was he who had contacted the banking institution at Oxford concerning a ransom. He had even given them the numbers, both of her accounts and of her numerical authorizations to access them. How he had obtained such numbers Kerensa had no idea, but the fact that he had most likely indicated a well-trained mind. Strangely, the thief apparently had no idea concerning her real wealth—the money inherited from her father.

Nevertheless, this kidnapping seemed well-planned, which would mean that Alistair would have formulated plans for after the ransom was paid and not simply for obtaining the money. He would know of the penalties of this sort of crime, and so he would be loathe to leave witnesses—any witnesses whatsoever. That, of course, would involve at least she and Wilford but would most likely also include poor Petroc and his foolish brother Neville, who would never imagine such treachery.

Still, it was another "what if" issue, one more thing for her to worry about. The one humorous aspect of the whole mess, though it was without doubt the most painful thing physically, actually made her want to laugh it was so ludicrous. The two brothers, after they had clubbed her over the head, had apparently dragged her up the narrow stairs to this room where they had secured her, not by ropes, but in what had to be the old stocks that had sat unused beneath the church's wagon-porch for the past two centuries or more. She was still in them, too, just like the old wags of former days, and the hours of being forced to kneel with her head almost at floor level and her neck extended between the old boards, as well as both her hands and wrists, was causing excruciating pain that was turning to a dangerous numbness. It was time, therefore, to effect some changes!

"There's something I think you brilliant criminals should be aware of," she breathed, making her voice weaker than it was, but finding it impossible to keep her sarcastic disdain to herself.

"Oh, she speaks now, she does. And I'll wager she's about to warn us about the great Joe Bloggs, who'll come smashing to her rescue at any moment. Don't you think that's what she's up to, Nev?"

"Oiaye, I do. And he might come if he wasn't so bloody dead, the poor bloke!"

"Or nearly so, anyway."

"Wilford may come and he may not," Kerensa declared icily. "If he does, it'll be you who has to deal with him. Of course you both know how well you've done against him in the past."

"Not today, Dr. Ren! Like I told you, we done him good today!"

"Yes, and he probably wasn't looking, either. Both of you are purse-snatching, back- stabbing cowards, and you know it! The next time you see him, however, you'll be facing him! Worse for you, he'll be ready! What happens to you then won't be pretty, I daresay. Still, I'd like very much being there to watch—"

"You won't be, you stupid old bird; not if you don't put a sock in it!"

"Temper, temper, Petroc. Remember the manners your mother taught you!"

"Oh, for—"

Kerensa did her best to smile. "But after all, boys, Wilford wasn't what I wished to speak with you about. Rather, it's what you are doing to me, and how Alistair is going to feel about it when he arrives and finds me dead and gone and still no ransom!"

"How'd she know about Alistair, Pet? How'd—"

"Shut up, Nev! And you, too, Dr. Ren. We ain't going to kill you—not yet, anway!"

"But you already are. Can't you see that these stocks were made to be set up on poles or boxes or something? They weren't made for use on the floor or ground. I don't know how many hours I've been kneeling all stooped and cramped the way you bound me, but I can tell you as a doctor that the numbness caused from my cut-off circulation has nearly reached my neck. Once it reaches my brain, then I'm dead, just like that. There'll be nothing either of you can do."

"Good! That'll serve you right for coming all over me so high and mighty! "

"Perhaps you are right. But Petroc, what Alistair forgot to tell you—or perhaps he doesn't want you to know—is that Oxford's financial institution has a policy of releasing no private funds without a direct-voice authorization. In other words, their computer has to hear my voice and match it through several code words before any money can be sent out!"

Actually Kerensa had no idea whether any of that was true. But it didn't take a genius to realize that most people could be duped by a little educated speech, especially if such speech pushed them in the direction their greed was already pulling them. Certainly these two were greedy enough—

"Pet, we got to put that thing up on some boxes or something!"

"I don't know, Nev. Alistair said all he needed was the numerical codes—"

"He was right, too," Kerensa interrupted again. "Numerical codes are required to get into the computer and then to open the accounts. It won't be long, however, until he calls, telling you to put me on the phone to the computer. That's the only way it can do a voice pattern analysis. Of course by then I'll most likely have expired—"

"Expired. That means dead, doesn't it?"

"Yeah, Nev, it means dead! All right, all right! Nev, go get a couple of chairs!"

"I'm going, Pet, but there ain't none except in the old chur—"

"Nev, you bloomin' nit! I told you not to say nothing about where we might happen to be!"

Again Kerensa smiled. "Don't worry, fellows. I already know we're in the Talland Church tower or steeple. I've known it from the moment we came through the doors downstairs."

"But…you were out cold as a cod! How—"

"I'm blind, remember? Blind people have their other senses expanded. I don't even know how it works, save that it does. Almost always I know exactly where I am, and where people around me are, too. For instance, Neville, right now you are standing on the top tread of the stair, while you, Petroc, are seated on a low box beside the ladder that goes up to the keep."

"Blimey, Pet, she's right!"

"Oh, shut your gob," Petroc ordered tiredly, "and go get the woman some bloody chairs!"

And Kerensa Tansin, knowing that she had finally won a round, if only a little one, began praying again that Wilford Abbott would somehow live.

Chapter Twenty-One

Whan Wilf, exhausted and dizzy from the incredibly steep climb, finally reached the top of the steps, he was once more in total darkness. He had no idea how high he'd climbed—ten feet, twenty feet, perhaps even thirty or forty feet. What he did know was that the steps were small and narrow, and they wound steeply up a near-vertical shaft or passageway that ended abruptly against a wooden structure that he sensed was a trapdoor set in a floor above.

There had been no protective railing on the stairs, so his laborious climb had been made while leaning away from the hole and against the cold rock sides of the shaft, the walking stick still helping him to keep his balance. And as he had climbed, he tried to clear his head, to think past the pain that seemed to envelope his entire being.

In agony, Wilf rested with his hand against the rough wood over his head, doing his level best to ignore his injuries, and meanwhile knowing full well that Kerensa was in trouble somewhere, and that he alone could save her! Yet already it might be too late! Those miserable punks might already have killed her, or worse! And even now he was not out of the old smugglers' hole, and had no real idea—

"Oh, dear God," he breathed with continued intensity, "please don't let this happen again! If she's still alive, please give me the strength to help her—"

Crowding himself up against the underside of the old door, Wilf began pushing with his back. At first nothing happened because he could only use his good leg and half his battered body, and twice he had to drop down two or three steps to ease the throbbing punishment he was taking. On his third try, however, he felt the door give slightly. A quantity of dust sifted down onto his head and the back of his neck, and as he stifled a cough, he wondered how Morwenna Miller had passed through it without disturbing the dust. A third time he strained against the heavy door, setting his teeth against the pain and willing his good leg to push harder. Suddenly something gave way, and a thin shaft of light streamed into the passageway.

Gasping and struggling to catch his breath, Wilf pushed again. Slowly the old door lifted up and shifted to the side. He had feared the grating of rusted hinges, but as it turned out the door had no hinges. Rather, it had been constructed to fit snugly into the opening in the floor, and once Wilf had crawled out and slid the door back into place, he could see no real sign of it whatsoever.

Pulling himself erect with the stick, he scuffed the dust around the uneven edges of the trapdoor just as the girl from the crossing must have done, and then he examined the dimly lit room. The structure, he could tell, was old, made of cut stone with a wooden stairway going up one wall. In the room were no windows, but one of the two double doors was ajar, and by that light and more filtering down the stairway from a room above, he quickly concluded that he had emerged into the church tower or steeple.

Amazed that he had managed to escape, Wilf was in the act of turning toward the open door when he heard, from above, the faint sound of Kerensa's voice. Thunderstruck, he stood motionless, willing her to speak again, praying and pleading. When she did, a moment later, Wilf did not hesitate but started up the stairs. Using his stick and the wall, he moved quietly and with caution, yet he was filled with a sense of urgency, a burning need to hurry that his body seemed utterly unable to comply with.

As his head cleared the floor of the room above, he saw that it was empty and that the stairs continued upward into yet another room, that one much better lit. There, he thought, he would see the three arched windows he had noted earlier. Which meant, his exhausted mind reminded him, that there was a door on this level—a door that opened to nothing but air.

Quickly he located it, but before he had time to see how it was secured, Kerensa's voice came again, more clearly. Though she was speaking quietly, Wilf could tell that she was entreating someone, trying to keep him from—

Petroc! She had to be alone up there with the lustful Petroc, and she was using all her wits and skill to stop him from hurting her.

Forgetting everything else, Wilf lunged up the stairs with no thought of being quiet. Every thought now was of Kerensa, poor blind Kerensa being held at the mercy of a merciless kid who had tried to murder him and was now focusing his evil intentions on her—

"That's enough!" he thundered as he pushed himself above the stair opening and into the room. Strangely, though Petroc had to have heard him coming, he did not even turn toward the stairs until the sound of Wilf's shouted order swivelled his head. Then he lurched guiltily from his knees to his feet, revealing to Wilf's stunned view the disheveled Kerensa, also on her knees but stooped down almost to the floor, her head and both hands locked securely in the heavy wooden beams of what had to be the church's missing stocks.

"Wilford," she exclaimed weakly as she tried to turn her head, but Wilf forced thought of her from his mind as he charged the startled Petroc.

"You miserable puke!" he growled as he lifted the old walking stick and struck the hapless young man, not swinging it but pushing it forward with his good hand and arm even as he was himself lunging forward. Petroc gasped and doubled over with pain as the end of the stick buried itself in his solar plexus, and before he could do more than blink, Wilf was on him, dropping the stick and using his one hand to hasten Patroc's downward momentum, smashing Orange-hair's wide-eyed, terrified face into his lifted knee, the one on the same leg as his bad ankle.

With a strange gurgle, Petroc dropped unconscious to the floor, blood gushing from his mouth and both his nostrils. In the act of pulling the Brit's body back upright to hit him again, Wilf saw that he was out and dropped him back. For a moment, he leaned with his hand and arm on the knee of his good leg, dragging in great gulps of air. Then, straightening, he hopped painfully to Kerensa's trembling form and dropped to his knees beside her.

"Wilford, dear," she gasped, struggling to breathe and to cry out at the same time, "you must watch out—"

"It's okay, Kerensa. I...I'm sorry it took me so long, but—"

"No, Wilford! No!"

"What?" Wilf questioned, trying to understand. "Petroc's out, Kerensa. You don't need to be afraid—"

"But you do, Joe Bloggs!"

Turning in surprise, Wilf realized he had forgotten all about Neville. He also realized that he had dropped his only weapon, for now the old stick was in the younger brother's hands, and already his vicious swing was in progress!

Instantly Wilf twisted his head to the side, just as if he were ducking a blow from his brother Heber's fist. He was surprisingly fast, too, but nowhere near fast enough. In the very next instant, the walking stick caught him hard behind his ear. Though the blow was glancing, it was wicked, and as pinpoints of light exploded inside Wilf's skull, he dropped onto the old stocks, his last sight before losing consciousness the shattered end of his stick spinning off against the wall. That, and a single tear rolling from beneath Kerensa Tansin's dark glasses and off her grimy cheek—

Chapter Twenty-Two

"Wiford, breathe! Try, Wilford dear. You must breathe more deeply! Please, Wilford. Breathe!"

As if from a distant fog, Wilf's mind began to clear, the raspy sound of Kerensa's voice echoing closely in his ear.

"Breathe, Wilford. That's it! Breathe deeply as you possibly can—"

"Ungh," he groaned as the pain washed over him once more, starting at his head and spreading downward like a searing blanket. But there was a change, too, his mind tried to tell him, something heavy pressing at his throat and squeezing his chest, his lungs—

"Wilford dear, do your best to breathe!"

His eyes popping open, Wilf felt the strangling around his neck and brought his hands—no, his good hand—up to pull away whatever it was...no, for some reason he couldn't bring up either hand! But his injured shoulder was screaming at him again—

"You're in the stocks, Wilford. Please listen to me. Neville locked your neck and wrists into the stocks, but they were made for much smaller people, and now you're being suffocated. Do you hear me?"

"I...hear...Where...are you—"

"Beside you, dear." Kerensa's voice was terribly raspy, and it dawned abruptly on Wilf that she was also suffering from lack of air.

"Are…is it too small for you?"

"No," the lovely social anthropologist replied quickly. "But Petroc bound me with my knees drawn up, and stooped over in this stocks as I am, I c…can't breathe well, and I've lost most of…of my circulation."

Trying to shake his head to clear it, Wilf found the locked-together beams so tight he couldn't turn his head. At the same time, however, he realized that the old stocks was not secured to the floor but could be lifted!

"Kerensa," he wheezed, "if I can somehow get my knees up under me and lift this thing off the floor, would that help you?"

"I…think so. But Wilford, darling, it is too heavy—"

No longer listening or even really thinking, Wilf hunched his body, trying to pull his knees up under his chest. He'd never tried such a thing without the use of his hands, and the weight of the stocks made it more difficult than ever. Then there was the unbelievable torture going on within his injured shoulder. Still, he finally drew the knee of his good leg up under him.

"Okay, Kerensa, now…lift!"

Straining together, the two captives managed, finally, to raise the heavy old beams off the floor. Hunching himself forward a fraction of an inch at a time, Wilf swung himself and his end of the stocks far enough around that it rested, finally, on the box Petroc had earlier been using as a chair. That made breathing a little easier, and though he could not see Kerensa at his side, the sound of her breathing also eased, and again hope began to grow in his heart.

"Is…it better?"

"M…much!" Kerensa breathed. "If I could…only get out of these awful ropes! I am…just so terribly numb—"

"Are you upright? At least on…on your knees?"

"I am, sort of."

"Until I can get to it, maybe this will…help the blood… flow better…What did they…What did Petroc…do to you—"

"Nothing, Wilford dear, except render me unconscious with a blow to the head. I...I don't know why I didn't hear them before they grabbed me. But I didn't, and they either dragged or carried me up to this room. Oh, they breathed a great many horrid threats, and once Petroc got Neville out of the room, he was going to...to—"

"Don't say any more, Kerensa. There's no need to!"

"But...that was when you came, darling! You stopped him! Somehow you always stop him! Oh, you poor dear, what have they done to you?"

"Not as...as much as they'd hoped, I imagine. They... dumped me into this old sepulcher, I guess it would be called, or stone vault, which was actually an opening into an underground cave."

"Smugglers!"

"Yeah, they called it a smugglers' hole. It must have been quite deep, though, because I really messed up my shoulder and ankle. But I landed in some sand, which is no doubt what saved my life. Oh, yeah, Petroc tried to stab me, too. But that's nothing, only a scratch. Anyway, I...I ended up here, I guess, and you know the rest. Where are they, by the way? Petroc and Neville?"

"I don't know what you did to Petroc, Wilford, but Neville was crying and working over him for the longest time. After Petroc started to come around, Neville kicked my head and told me not to move—"

"He'll pay for that, Kerensa. I promise!"

"Of course he will, and it isn't worth worrying about, anyway. Then he locked you in beside me and helped his brother down the stairs. They haven't been back."

"But...why would they leave?"

"Neville was mumbling something about Alistair and the telephone. Alistair is someone who is with them in this scheme."

"I heard his name when they first hit me, out in the graveyard. I...I fell asleep, Kerensa, and I know that's when they grabbed you. If only I had stayed awake! If only—"

"My darling Wilford, it's all right. We're here together, and now it doesn't even seem to matter any more."

"But...it *does* matter! I...I can't bear...to lose...anyone else—"

"Wilford, please."

"Kerensa," Wilf pleaded, an ancient agony in his voice, "you...don't understand! My baby sister, Missy? I killed her! Me! And with her I killed my folks just as certainly!"

"You killed your sister?" Kerensa was thunderstruck. "No, Wilford, you couldn't have! That isn't who you are! I know it isn't!"

"I...I didn't mean it to happen, and that's God's own truth! It really was an accident! Only...only I—" For a moment Wilf fought his emotions, fighting to control his voice. "Mother was always right," he finally breathed, starting in from a different direction, "only I didn't believe it. I don't know why I was so full of doubt and rebellion, unless it was that I was sixteen and desperately anxious to be as adult as Annie and my two older brothers. So I argued with her about everything, and defied her whenever I could!"

For a moment Wilf struggled with his emotions, something very new to him, for he had always prided himself on keeping them under control.

"Wilford," Kerensa misunderstood, "please don't try to speak if you can't get air for your lungs."

"It...isn't that. My breathing is okay. It...it's just...so difficult to talk about all this...stuff! Dad wasn't home that day—it seemed as though he was *never* home when we needed him—and for some reason I had decided it was up to me to stop Mother from ruining Melissa, who was nine and spoiled so rotten nobody could stand being near her. I mean, she got away with everything she attempted, and Mother seemed blind to it."

For a long moment Wilf was silent, his eyes glazed with pain. "We were an Arizona ranching family," he finally continued, "and a lot of our work had to be done on horseback. For all of us but Melissa, riding had become pretty much second nature. Missy balked at it, claiming to be afraid of horses, and Mother didn't force the issue like she had with the rest of us. Neither did Dad when he was around."

"Your mother forced all of you to learn to ride?"

Momentarily forgetting the stocks, Wilf tried to look at Kerensa but couldn't. "I...didn't mean it that way. I meant that through the years she had forced all of us to do things we feared or found distasteful. Once when I was scared of an old bull, Mother assigned me the care of it for that entire summer." Briefly Wilf grimaced at the memory. "Needless to say, by the end of the summer that bull was running from me.

"The trouble was, claiming fear of horses meant Missy could avoid her share of the work, which was always charted out in our kitchen so we knew what we had to do. It also meant that one of the rest of us had to pick up the slack, which all of us thought was unfair.

"That day Mother was in the house when Missy started taunting Julie about not riding fence—"

"Riding fence?" Kerensa asked, trying to understand.

"Yeah," Wilf grimaced, "checking our fenceline to see that it was up and secure—you know, to keep our small herd of cows from straying. Missy and Julie had the assignment that Saturday, and I happened to come out of the barn just as Missy was taunting Julie with her old, 'You can't make me or I'll tell Mother!' routine.

"Well, Julie was exercising wonderful patience, but I lost it. I mean, I lost my temper. It wasn't like I was the one who had to go instead of her or anything like that. It was just that I was so blasted tired of Missy getting away with things and lording it over the rest of us the way she did, that I took matters into my own hands.

"Grabbing her, I whacked her a good one on the seat of her jeans, started cussing a blue streak when she bit me on the arm, and then I literally threw her onto the back of the old horse Julie had saddled for her.

"Screaming, Missy tried to slide off the other side, and that *really* upset me. Grabbing her leg I yanked her back into the saddle, held it so she couldn't kick me, and then I stuck her boot into the stirrup and yelled at her to leave it there or I'd whack her another one—this time where it would do some good.

"Missy stopped trying to kick me and started whimpering and trembling—actually shaking—begging me to let her off the horse. She'd claimed to be afraid of horses for a long time—I guess all her life. And all her life she had acted like she was afraid of them. But despite her pleas, I forced her to stay in the saddle.

"About then Julie grabbed my arm and started telling me that we hadn't ought to force Missy to ride before she was ready."

For a moment Wilf paused, his eyes closed and his forehead beaded with sweat, and Kerensa could tell he was back in Arizona, reliving once again his horrid nightmare.

"The thing was, I hadn't ever seen Missy tremble the way she was, and it scared me so bad I was thinking of pulling her out of the saddle and letting her go. Only I'd seen a western movie once, about a little kid being taught to swim by being thrown into a deep pond, and I remember thinking that's what needed to happen with Missy. All she needed was somebody willing to force her to ride, and then in a few minutes she'd be riding just fine, and we wouldn't have any more problems with her.

"When Julie grabbed my arm and took Missy's side, I lost my temper again. I grabbed Julie's hand and threw it away from my arm, spinning her around I was so furious, and she accidentally fell against the flank of Missy's horse.

"I don't know if the animal was already excited because of all the yelling and screaming everybody was doing, but when Julie slammed into it and then fought to regain her balance, the old horse went berserk. It literally bolted into the air, snapping its reins where Julie had tied them to the pole fence. Then it started sunfishing or spinning in the air just like a rodeo mount will sometimes do, and Julie and I just stared.

"The next thing either of us knew, the horse was standing quiet and trembling on the other side of the corral, and Mother was running out of the house wailing a strangled sort of cry, and Melissa was on the ground next to the fence, looking all still and silent."

Wilf took a long, labored breath. "It...it turned out that her neck had snapped, leaving her like a...little rag doll—"

Kerensa's face was white. "Oh, Wilford," she breathed, "I am so sorry."

"Yeah," Wilf muttered bitterly. "So have I been—every minute of my miserable life since then! But what good does sorry do, Kerensa, especially when you've killed your baby sister? Try, sometime, and make that go away with an apology!"

"I...know," Kerensa replied, her raspy voice suddenly subdued, almost wooden. "Oh, Wilford, dear, how I know!"

And then silence returned to the ancient upper room.

Chapter Twenty-Three

"*T*here's no way you can understand," Wilf murmured as he struggled to adjust his neck between the old boards. Why, he was wondering, was he always so open with this woman? Why couldn't he just learn to keep his mouth shut? One of these days, he felt certain, it was all going to come back to haunt him—

"Can't I, Wilford? How much do you know about me? Really."

"I...don't...Not much, I guess. But I'm not as good as you at asking questions, either."

Through her cracked lips, and despite their desperate situation, Kerensa laughed. "I have been a bit unfair, haven't I. But now let me tell you a little. Though I never admit this to anyone, I was born in Chicago—"

"You aren't British?" Wilf was astounded.

"I am now, and of course from my name one can surmise that one or both of my parents—in my case it happened to be my father—had a Cornish background. Several generations ago his family dwelt in the Kilminorth Woods, just outside Looe. When they left, they emigrated to America, to Chicago. It was there my father met and married my mother, after which I was brought into the world, followed two years later by my younger sister. We two were all the children they had.

"Meanwhile, Father was doing very well financially. He had a huge office on the Chicago Loop and a mansion on the North Side, as well as vacation homes in both Colorado and Massachusetts, with his own private plane to carry he and his equally wealthy guests back and forth from one to another. Very quickly, you see, he and Mother were moving up in the world.

"Unfortunately, they became obsessed with their new social status; and the nuances of climbing socially, with all its subtle and not-so-subtle selfishness, arrogance and deceit, became the only values my sister and I were taught when we were small.

"When I was eleven, Mother was killed by a drunken driver, and while Father was in hospital recovering, our governess placed my sister and me in separate boarding schools and then took off with one of my parents' lawyers."

"Why not the same boarding school?" Wilf questioned.

"Our age differences. The cut-off age at my school was ten, so my nine-year-old sister couldn't attend. Anyway, when he was released from the hospital, Father decided to leave us there, and it wasn't long before he was married again—to an exceptionally beautiful woman who had a heart like flint. Father was her ticket to the good life, you see, and if anything, she was more socially adept than my mother.

"Her only real dilemma, as it turned out, was us. The first time we came home after their marriage, I led out in devious but childish little plots and schemes against her, for I didn't want her thinking she was my mother. In less than a week the woman had made such a fuss over what we had done, and created so much misery for my father, that we were sent away again—to year-round boarding schools. That...that was the last time I ever saw my sister!"

"What?" Wilf questioned in amazement. "What happened? Did she die?"

"No, we were just kept separated. Neither of us was ever allowed home again, and by age sixteen I had completely stopped corresponding with her. I remember thinking of her as an immature, spoiled brat, and I'm certain she thought worse of me."

For a moment Kerensa grew silent, and Wilf, trying to comprehend all he had been hearing, was now aching for the woman at his side. How fortunate he had been, he found himself thinking, to grow up in such a close-knit family—close-knit in spite of what had happened to little Missy.

"Sixteen years of age seems to have been traumatic for both of us," he finally breathed.

Kerensa tried to smile her agreement. "More than you know, Wilford. The last time I saw my father was also when I was sixteen, when he flew in for the Coming-out Ball the school held each year for we spoiled little debutantes. It was a disastrous night, for both of us, and when he left he never returned."

"You're right," Wilf acknowledged quietly. "What a terrible tragedy to endure at such a youthful age! I don't know how I'd keep going if it weren't for my family!"

"You would, just like I did."

Soberly Wilf nodded. "I imagine. So, where are they now? Your father and sister, I mean."

"Both dead," Kerensa replied almost matter-of-factly. "Father and his wife got some bad dope at one of their famous social functions—either that, or they just plain overdosed. I've heard both, and I can't seem to make myself care which it was! The point is that they died, and in that moment my sister and I became filthy rich."

"The money Petroc and company are after, I assume?"

"Actually, I don't believe they even know about it. All they are after, apparently, is my hundred thousand pounds plus of savings held at Oxford—that, and perhaps some sort of ransom they hope the University will pay for my release. At least those are the only numbers I've heard them discuss. Only, none of it makes any sense! This kidnapping has to have been planned for a long time, Wilford. It takes time to set up places of security, like this old church tower, for instance. But why would they go to so much trouble, and risk so much, for such a paltry sum of money?

"Another thing about this that doesn't add up. I only made the decision to work in Cornwall a little over three weeks ago, and I didn't announce it to anyone until I placed that advert for an assistant."

"In the newspaper?"

"That is correct."

"That's probably how they knew, then."

"Perhaps, but it doesn't give them enough time, besides which I keep my account numbers so secret that nobody knows them! And there are other things I shan't mention. All together, Wilford, it feels almost as though someone else was to be the real victim, and I was taken either by accident or as an afterthought—one or the other."

"I don't know, Kerensa. I thought I came here almost by accident, too."

"Perhaps, then, there are no accidents?"

"That's what my folks thought." Wilf was doing his best to blink the salt-sting of sweat and blood from his eyes, and to keep the pain in his shoulder from overwhelming his mind. "'There's a plan governing everything,' they used to say. And…and your sister? How did she pass away?"

"Truthfully, Wilford, I don't know. Perhaps it was drugs like my father. I suppose she might also have been murdered, for her occasional letters indicated she was living very expensively, very dangerously. Then again, perhaps she merely died from a lonely, broken heart—like I almost did." Kerensa sighed heavily. "I really don't know. I didn't even hear about her passing for three years after the fact, and then I didn't get any details."

Wilf was surprised that there was no trace of bitterness in Kerensa's voice. His own bitterness and self-loathing over the death of little Melissa had very nearly destroyed him. Of course Kerensa had no reason to blame herself the way he had been doing, but still—

"The upshot of all this," Kerensa was continuing, her voice quiet, "is that now I'm alone, Wilford, totally alone! There have been days when I've felt so miserable and lonely that it has been hard to find a reason for not taking my own life. To be honest about it, it was at sixteen that I began fighting those feelings, too."

"I am so sorry, Kerensa. I…I've been pretty disdainful of you, at least in some ways, but I had no idea—"

"Wilford, dear, you have no reason to apologize. I gave you no chance to know. I feel as though I have been such a coward about my past, about my life—"

"Sshh!" Wilford interrupted urgently, his voice a low whisper. "There's someone on the stairs!"

"But, how can you—"

"Sshh!"

In agony the two waited, their bent backs toward the stair opening, their minds running rampant with all sorts of terrible possibilities. Wilf had never felt so helpless! Even in the depths of the cave he had been able to move about. But now he was secured in the heavy stocks, and he could literally feel the stealthy approach of someone who was already coming across the floor behind him and Kerensa—

"Don't cry out!" a feminine voice whispered fiercely. "I have the key, but if they hear anything, they'll be up here in a flash!"

"Who…are you?"

"A friend, I suppose you might say. A very sorry friend."

Wilf could hear the woman working the key in the lock on the stocks, though still he could see nothing of her.

"I…was watching, mister, when Petroc and Neville clubbed you in the graveyard. It was sickening, but then when they dumped you in that terrible hole—"

"It…can't be!" Wilf breathed, his heart suddenly pounding. "I don't believe—"

The lock clicked open, seconds later the ancient beam was lifted off the necks and wrists of Wilf and Kerensa, and as Wilf straightened his back and turned around to face his rescuer, he was not at all surprised to see the enticing form of a uniform-clad school girl, her dark and radiant hair tumbling down over her shoulders.

Kerensa, still bound, turned her head and gasped at the sight of the girl, but Wilf said nothing, made no sound. So, he was thinking, this at long last was Morwenna Miller! And she was just as he had seen, had imagined! He had even heard the sound of her voice!

Yet, there was something about her that wasn't quite right—

"Morwenna?" he breathed, his own voice caught in his throat. "Are...you Morwenna Miller?"

"Blimey, no!" the woman whispered as she pulled off her wig of dark hair. "Though that's who I've made me up to look like, all right!"

"You...you've been acting the part of Morwenna Miller?"

"I have," the woman answered as she deftly cut the rope that had bound Kerensa, "most every day since this past Christmas, at least when conditions was gloomy or misty enough! Now hurry, the both of you, or they'll suss me out sure and we'll all be dead—"

"Wait a moment," Kerensa questioned as she did her best to rub circulation back into her legs. "Why have you...they, I mean, been doing this?"

"For the money, naturally." The woman grinned knowingly. "After the Miller girl died, Alistair found out about her gobs of money, so ever since he's been keeping his eye on her grave, waiting for her relatives to show up and claim her."

"What...was he going to do?"

"I don't know, Dr. Tansin. He had some brilliant scheme all cooked up, that's certain. Only no one ever came. Finally this past winter, he and Petroc decided to bring out her ghost—meaning me, of course—and since then they've been spreading word of her haunts all over the country. They figured that'd get her relations stirred up, sure! They hired me to play the ghost—offered me five hundred quid—to be paid after they'd collected from the relations. I was fool enough to believe the scheme might actually succeed!"

"So, it's been you I've seen?" Wilf was practically dizzy he was so astounded.

She nodded. "I was in the graveyard when they hit you, if that's want you mean. Other than that, I don't know. Without getting caught, I've been doing my best to be seen by as many people as possible. Now, can either of you stand upright? I'm stronger than I look, so I can assist."

"Why are you helping us?"

"They never said a word about hurting or killing, is why! That isn't my way, and when I saw it, I started right then searching for a way to assist you. Thing is, mister, when you went head-first into that awful hole, I never figured to see you again. Then when I heard from Neville you was up here and had pounded that randy Petroc in the gut so hard he nearly died; well, that did my poor heart good, it did. That cheeky bloke's raped me, he has! Twice! And me with no good way to get even!"

"Wait a minute! You just said—"

"Not now! There's a door in the room below that goes out to nowhere. I found a ladder and got up to it from the outside, and that's how I got past those blokes at the bottom. The door opens to the outside, which I thought strange, and it wasn't even latched. I don't know why. Once there may have been another room there, or a stairs, perhaps. We can go back out through it and down the ladder, but we have to go quiet, and fast!"

"Who are you?"

"Daisy. Daisy Pencarrow."

"Why does every name in Cornwall start with *Pen*?" Wilf growled as Daisy helped him to his feet. "Penryn, Penzance, now Pencarrow—"

"Haven't you heard the old ditty?" Daisy whispered as she turned to assist Kerensa.

When you hear Tre, Pol or Pen,
Know you've met a Cornishman!

"*Tre* in old Cornish means 'town,'" she continued, carrying on as though Wilf and Kerensa were truly concerned about such things and had made a dozen inquiries. Of course, Wilf thought with disgust, he had opened the ball—

"*Pol* is 'pool,' and *pen* means 'end' or edge of something. Penpol, then, means end of pool, and Trepenpol would be town at the end of the pool." Daisy giggled almost soundlessly. "Of course it doesn't always work. My old man says Pencarrow means hill of the stag, but I think it means end of the stag, for none have been seen near our place in a hundred years and more!

"Now, are we all quite ready?"

Wilf rolled his eyes behind the endlessly nattering woman, though Kerensa's sweet smile kept him from saying anything.

"Right, right," Daisy went on as though she had been answered. "Now we must hurry!"

Arms draped over or about each other for mutual support, Wilf, Kerensa and Daisy Pencarrow shuffled across the room and started down the stairs. They were steep and narrow, but Daisy went first, acting as a support for Wilf and Kerensa, who hobbled along behind. Kerensa's circulation had been only partially restored, so she was having nearly as much difficulty as Wilf. But for some reason he was feeling a little better, a little stronger. Yes, he had a pounding in his head that was almost blinding, and his left shoulder and ankle still throbbed mercilessly. Still, now that the mystery of Morwenna Miller had been solved—

But had it? Wilf realized in an instant that he really didn't know. Had this been the girl who had appeared in the smugglers' cave, or in Polperro, or at the crossing? From this woman's eyes there had been absolutely no communication, yet on each of the other occasions the feeling from whomever he had seen had been almost overwhelming! Besides, it had taken only a glance to see that Daisy's eyes were not the same amazing blue! So, who or what had he seen—

"Very good," the woman breathed as they moved off the stairs. "There's the door, and all we have ahead is to get you both out and down the ladder."

Chapter Twenty-Four

"**W**here do you nits think you're going?" The harsh sound of Petroc's whiney voice stopped them where they stood and, turning, Wilf quickly pushed the two women away. "That's it, Petroc," he growled as he turned his good side toward the sneering, would-be murderer. "I'm sick and tired of you two circus-freak brothers bashing me over the head and waving your skinny little knives at me! Whatever else happens here, you're finished!"

"Righto," Petroc grinned evilly as he pulled out his switchblade and dropped into his familiar but foolish-looking crouch, his eyes never leaving Wilf's face. "Don't you go anywhere, Daisy, me luv. It's soon time you learned how turncoats are dealt with here in Cornwall." He was snarling at the woman but not looking at her. Instead his eyes were as burning coals, trying to consume Wilf with their hatred. "Now, American," he continued, "what're you going to do? Neville says you have one arm and one leg that ain't worth salt, and I can see from here your head's half caved in. Seems to me your smalls'd be bunched pretty tight, Joe Bloggs, since any second now I'll be slicing you up into ribbons—"

Petroc was right, and Wilf knew it. He had no idea what he was going to do. Worse, even if he'd been able to think of something, he doubted whether his body had the strength to accomplish it. His dizziness and pounding headache were back, there was no way his ankle could stand more than maybe another few seconds' weight, his shoulder felt like it was being hit with a shotgun blast with every tiny movement, and the gash on his forehead was bleeding again, getting blood into his one eye. In short, Wilf knew he was in mighty sorry shape! And now this miserable orange-haired punk was back in his face! It was—

"Wilford, dear," Kerensa whispered urgently, "don't fight him, please; just avoid him!"

"She's right, luv," Daisy added with a whisper of her own, "just stay out of his way, and leave the ugly bloke to us!"

"I'm not letting him hurt you," Wilf breathed back as he tried to focus on Petroc's eyes, "either of you!"

"He won't, Wilford. Just please keep away from his knife—"

"Whispering about me, are we?" Petroc sneered again. Then with an exaggerated lunge he feinted a charge, lifted his knife, and went to work. "Stupid American!" he snarled, his blade now far forward and swishing viciously back and forth. "My throat's already seen that fancy trick of yours, but now you ain't got fingers left to try it again."

Only then did the overly-anxious Petroc realize that Wilf had not raised his hand toward his throat at all and was *not* recoiling in horror as his outstretched fingers took the brunt of the knife. Instead he was standing motionless, both hands intact and at his sides, a slight smile playing on his battered face.

"So long, Orange-hair."

"What?" Petroc was still staring in wonder at his bloodless switchblade, and from there to Wilf's perfectly healthy fingers. "Oiaye, Joe Bloggs!" he whined as his eyes slid back to Wilf's smiling face, "You ain't gobbing me again!"

His face suddenly contorted with fury, Petroc threw himself into a true lunge, hurling himself with all his might in the general direction of this immovable American who so stubbornly refused to die. His hand with the switchblade was lower now, in perfect position to slash and disembowel. His other hand was open and tense, ready to grab any part of Wilf or his clothing and draw him close where the cutting could begin in earnest.

At last, he was thinking! This was how it should be—face to face at the time of killing! The American, too frightened to do anything else, would recoil to the very spot where Petroc wanted him, where he could most easily turn and pinion him against the wall. At the same time, Dr. Ren remained somewhere behind him, screaming in fear—which was good, he thought, brilliant, as she would be the next to die. Then he would take care of the treacherous Daisy Pencarrow, who was—

As suddenly as that, Wilf took one hop away from where Petroc had expected, away from where he himself would have dodged to avoid his reaching blade. More surprising to the orange-haired one, the American's hands remained at his sides, not coming up, not defending himself the way he should have—

Petroc, in that fraction of a second when he realized he was going to miss Wilf badly and was already drawing up to turn back, was nevertheless astounded! How could the man do that? How could he remain so calm in the face of the deadly knife? And how was it that he seemed always just a fraction of an inch beyond Petroc's fearsome grasp? No matter, though, the much-pierced and torn young man thought with sly humor as he began an effortless spin with his blade still at the ready. The sorry fool had no weapon.

A sudden, heavy weight smashed violently into Petroc's back, knocking him forward, and over his shoulder the startled and still non-comprehending Penryn brother was astounded to glimpse the famous Dr. Kerensa Tansin, her face reflecting her fury as she pulled back and away from where she had shoved him. She had not been screaming in fear, he realized in that instant, but rather her wild scream had been an almost primordial battle-cry as she rose up to defend her man.

But now Petroc was stumbling forward with the impetus of Kerensa's shove, further past the American and toward the wall—no, toward the old door. But that was all right, he grinned evilly, for in another instant he would be stopped and turned back around—"

"Ummph!" he gasped as another weight slammed into him from behind, this one actually hurting it hit so hard. "Daisy!" he gasped as he lifted his hand to stop himself at the old door. He had also glimpsed her stony countenance, the ugly bird, so it had indeed been his former confederate in crime. Well, good for her, the cheeky fool! Now he had even better reason to do her—after he was finished with the other two, of course.

Petroc was at the door then, still stumbling hard ahead. But his hand was up to stop himself, and in another second—

The ever-scheming young man's hand touched the door, he pushed gleefully against it to set himself and his blade for the murderous time of his young life, and the door swung soundlessly open to the outside, giving way before him. Then the orange-haired former assistant to the famous social anthropologist of a sudden found himself dropping his knife and flailing wildly at the doorframe and then at the open air with both grasping hands!

In a span of time that seemed to last forever, he actually felt his feet carry him stumbling across the ancient threshold. Below him there was nothing but a rapidly-receding twenty-foot ladder with two coppers on it gaping up at him, and then all he could see was a jumbled but threatening assortment of tall old monuments to the dead, most of them with pointed stone or iron crosses rising menacingly from their tops. But that was just fine and dandy, his twisted but ever-hopeful mind was doing its best to convince him, for somehow he was airborne but not falling! He was—

And then, as the armed old monuments seemed suddenly to rush upward, from the depths of Petroc's dark and ugly soul there came a hideous but mercifully short-lived scream.

Chapter Twenty-Five

"*H*ello, old top!" Clive, ever the gregarious host, was in fine form though the occasion wasn't exactly his to take charge of. Still, Wilf noted as he came slowly down the stairs, nobody seemed to be arguing with the elderly hero. "Well, my goodness!" he gushed on, "Kerensa looks lovely as always; this new waif in the odd school attire radiates a certain happiness; but you, my dear boy, look very much the worse for wear!"

Wincing as he led Kerensa and Daisy off the steps and onto the lower floor of the old tower, the floor that cleverly hid the ancient trapdoor, Wilf did his best to smile. "Good to see you, too, Clive. Even better to see that you brought the cavalry!"

"Yes, lovely of me, wasn't it!" Clive grinned widely, then lowered his voice. "Took a bit of sussing out, I admit, with practically forced admittance to the privacy of a certain lovely young woman's bungalow at Granite Henge. But once I discerned your proper whereabouts and knew that evil was afoot, why, it took little to galvanize the sergeant here, as well as his lovely assortment of brave men and true."

Clive smiled widely. "Of course it helped immeasurably when I happened to mention that I am a true hero of the Second Great War—one of the few left around to be appropriately worshiped, as I so aptly put it. He at once could see my point, hastened to stir up his troops, and tally ho, my dear boy! Here we are!"

"Yeah, yeah, yeah!" Wilf smiled through his pain and exhaustion. "Clive, I'd like you to meet our 'Morwenna Miller.' She's been helping Kerensa and me to make our escape! Turns out she's a little better known as Daisy Pencarrow."

"Daisy Pencarrow, is it? Well, girl, you gave my Ann quite the fright the other eve, when you made your appearance at the crossing."

"At the crossing?" Daisy looked confused. "But sir, I don't—"

"Terras Bridge, my dear girl, where the true Morwenna Miller perished these ten years since."

"I...I am sorry, sir," Daisy stammered, her eyes wide with sudden understanding, "but I absolutely refused all appearances near that spot! Too many chances of running into the real thing, one might say. If your Ann or anyone else saw Morwenna Miller lingering about that dreadful crossing, then you'll have to look to her ghost for an explanation."

"Hear, hear," Clive muttered as he watched the young woman being led away by a uniformed officer. "It seems, dear Wilford, as if our little mystery remains intact."

"Perhaps, though more and more I'm coming to believe—"

"Clive," Kerensa interrupted, at the same time taking Wilf by the arm, "how did you find us? How did you know where to look? Or even that we were in trouble?"

"Why, Kerensa, my dear, when we found the Mercedes in the car park at Granite Henge, and the both of you missing—"

"The Mercedes was at Granite Henge?" Wilf questioned in surprise.

"And where else would it be, dear boy? Though why the two of you should have walked all the way here to the Talland Church in the awful fog we had this morning, would puzzle even the best of minds!"

Shaking his head, Wilf could only stare at Kerenza. "Petroc or Neville?" she suggested hopefully. "Or maybe Alistair, whomever he is?"

"Beats me, Kerensa. I still have the keys in my pocket, though of course Petroc may have had an extra made before you fired him."

"But...he had no time!"

"Then I don't know," Wilf shrugged. "Thing is, why would they want to take it back to Granite Henge in the first place? Surely they'd have known it would give the alarm!"

Now shaking her own head, Kerensa turned again to their loquacious benefactor, pushing aside her fear of what her next question might reveal. "Another thing, Clive. How...did you know that we had...come here to the old church?"

"My dear girl," the elderly military hero replied dourly, "you are the one who left on your table the thoroughly detailed schedule for today. And a fine work it was, I must say! We had only to follow it, the police and I, and we were led directly to you."

Again Kerensa was shaking her head. "I...I made no such schedule, Clive. Our coming here today was entirely spontaneous, prompted wholly by the density of the fog."

"But...but," and now even Clive seemed astounded, "those other fellows of most evil mein; they also found you! If no one knew you were coming here, how in heaven's name did they manage?"

Abruptly Kerensa smiled. "Well, at least that one's simple. Petroc knew I would be coming here sooner or later, for I had told him so immediately upon his arrival. I just didn't tell him when, for I hadn't yet decided. When I finally got my senses back, Neville told me they'd been waiting two days and were glad I'd finally arrived."

"Speaking of Petroc, Clive," Wilf interjected, "the police will find him in the portion of the graveyard east of the tower— dead, more than likely."

"Yes," Clive nodded solemnly, "two of the officers hastened in with the tale only moments ago. Seems they'd had a vision of sorts, a screaming, orange-haired angel who had no effective wings, but who quite miraculously at the last moment sprouted out from between his shoulder-blades the top several inches of a stout iron cross."

"So, he is dead," Kerensa breathed with relief.

"Indubitably so, my dear child. It would seem our friend Petroc has been literally impaled by Christianity."

"Well," Wilf agreed laconically, "at least it's one less heathen for good Christian Cornishmen to contend with."

"Quite right, old top. Neither will he be troubling lovely young social anthropologists any longer!" Pausing, Clive glanced out the double door and under the wagon porch. "Ah, yes. I might also report that Petroc's faithful brother Neville has been singing like the proverbial canary—a most lengthy and doleful tune of such numerous and varied foul and nefarious deeds that it will take the police years, running to ground the clues.

"The other news, of course—and this I was told by the sergeant only a moment or so before you appeared on the steps with your two ladies, Wilford—is that they have a fine bead drawn on the identity of the secretive but authoritative fellow known as Alistair, whom Neville has also described in some detail. In fact, some of the police spotted him nearby only moments ago, and I should guess—well, jolly good! Here they come now. I believe, dear boy, that you will enjoy renewing old acquaintances."

Having no idea what his elderly and far too verbose friend was talking about, Wilford was looking for a place to sit down, or even collapse, if necessary, when a group of police silently marched up the stairs and into the room. Glancing at them, Wilf nodded a greeting to the only one he knew— the policeman he had met that first day on the station platform at Liskeard.

"So you have him, I see?" the officious sergeant grilled one of the others. "Good, good. Well, Alistair McCoomber, what have you to say for yourself? Acting all the time as if you're concerned for the kin of a dead child, and the entire time it's their money you've been after. Stealing evidence, too—the poor girl's clothes and everything else she'd left that you could get your polluted hands on. Even cashing in her travelers cheques, which makes you nothing more than a common thief!

"Then when that scheme failed, instead of giving up and doing your proper work like an honest bloke, you went after what you thought was second best—kidnaping for ransom the finest social anthropologist on our Isle today. I know, for I've read her work, and I adore it. For shame, Alistair McCoomber! Especially because the poor woman turns out to be blind and helpless as a kitten. A fine and trusted officer you've turned out to be! While the murderous Petroc Penryn is mouldering in his grave, you and your other confidant in crime, foolish young Neville Penryn, whom the records show you've freed without authority a dozen times over, will soon be counting off together the years in the dungeons on Bodmin Moor.

"Men, make certain those cuffs are tight!"

And to Wilf's amazement, the cuffs were tightened on the arms of the very police officer he had turned Petroc and Neville over to that day in Liskeard so long, it seemed, before.

"Well, my good man," Clive beamed as he took Wilf's arm, "it's off to hospital with you and our dear Kerensa. They'll go over you both with a fine-toothed comb—"

"Then…there are no others Kerensa needs to fear?" Wilf gazed in wonder at his elderly friend. "No one else in the plot, as they say?"

"Nary a one, dear boy. In dashing style, you've vanquished them all!"

At Kerensa's smile, Wilf rolled his eyes. Would the old soldier never stop with his sarcastic embellishments? "What about statements to the police?" he pressed.

"All in due time, Wilford. They'll know where to find you." Clive's tender smile betrayed his love and concern, which he tried with great finesse and humor to keep hidden.

"Now, my dear friends, neither of you exhibits a picture of perfect health. Therefore, may I have the privilege of escorting you immediately to the waiting ambulance?"

And, smiling together but for three different reasons altogether, the friends exited the old tower.

Wilf had always supposed that the greatest battles he would ever fight would be physical, against the forces of evil and injustice. Maybe that was because of all his mother had told him, and maybe it was because he was still too young to know better. No matter, he was now coming face to face with the truth. The greatest battles he would ever wage—for that matter, that most of us will ever wage—would be within the confines of his own heart. There he would be forced to choose between two versions of right, two views of goodness. Was he to follow his own desires and yearnings, or was he to follow the spiritual force his mother had so carefully introduced him to? In this case, was he to give his heart to Kerensa Tansin or Morwenna Miller? The choice was now before him.

Only two things complicated the matter. He hadn't been able to find Morwenna Miller, and he'd received absolutely no divine witness regarding Kerensa Tansin....

Chapter Twenty-Six

*T*he May sun was streaming through the window of the room where Wilf lay, warming him and giving him the feeling of never wanting to move his body again. For three days and four nights, he'd been probed and scanned and shot and stitched and bound and cleaned and rebound—Well, the upshot was that he still felt tired, and from time to time had to fight even to keep his eyes open.

In all that time he hadn't seen Kerensa, though from members of her "staff," whatever that meant, he knew she had been discharged after the first night. Wilf's condition being enough worse to warrant a more lengthy stay, his room, compliments of Kerensa and her staff, was now awash with flowers and candies and almost nauseatingly sweet notes of goodwill. He'd even had to finally throw out two of her staff—two very proper gentlemen who had become so overbearing in their insistence on seeing to his every need that he had about lost his mind.

For the past hour or so it had been quiet, however, and so Wilf had been stirring about in his mind, pushing aside thoughts of the incredibly lovely Kerensa Tansin and her apparently obscene amount of money so he could focus on the real problem of his life—Morwenna Miller!

There was absolutely no doubt in Wilf's mind that the Lord had both heard and asnwered the prayer he had offered up in the smugglers' cave. Not only had Morwenna Miller showed up to reveal to him the hidden stairs, but everything else Wilf had pleaded for had been granted. Therefore, the girl had to be real!

But what did that mean? Real to God? Real to him? Real to her family, like the woman Daisy Pencarrow would surely be, though she could have no part of his own reality? It had all become so confusing, and no matter how he stirred things around in his head, he couldn't seem to feel any peace.

All he knew, in fact, was that Daisy had been the Morwenna Miller of the old graveyard, for she had admitted it without knowing he had even seen her. He also knew that the Morwenna Miller of the crossing had *not* been Daisy. Neither had she been the one in front of the pasty shop in Polperro. That the ever-talkative Daisy had chattered on about while they had been descending the old stairs following Petroc's final plunge, declaring to him and Kerensa that she had never "appeared" in Polperro because of the steep, narrow streets that would make escape too difficult. And again, because the comment had been unsolicited, Wilf believed her.

The other thing he knew, the most perplexing thing, was that the Morwenna Miller of the crossing, of the shop window in Polperro, and of the old smugglers' cave, had communicated with him in a silent but most wondrous manner, exactly as his mother had promised that she would. Somehow, without speaking a word, that Morwenna Miller had conveyed to him the certainty that she alone was his long-awaited and desperately longed-for eternal companion and mate.

Unbidden thoughts of his mother then filled Wilf's mind. From his earliest teenage years she had singled him out, separating him from his brothers and sisters with the quietly-uttered promise that if he would save himself in purity—the same sort of purity Clive and Ann Payne had spoken of so fervently—he would one day meet and know in the same instant that he had found his one true love. Moreover, his mother's promise had continued, the young woman would know it, too, and each of them would have the knowledge that they had truly come home at last.

It had been a unique promise, one he had never really spoken of with anyone, though he had pried enough into the experiences of his brothers and sisters to know they had been given no such exact counsel. Once he had shared a little of it with Brig, early on, and had been laughed at for his troubles. From that moment, he had begun to doubt it for himself, and in the doubting, which had been augmented by the harsh and difficult experiences of Missy's and his parents' deaths, he had grown to doubt and reject everything else his mother had ever told him.

Yet now it had happened—the very thing she had promised. Or anyway, half of it had. Because it had happened with a ghost or troubled spirit or extremely elusive woman that he could never seem to bring into a conversation, he had no idea if she had felt a thing! Worse, now the incredibly lovely Kerensa Tansin had managed to worm her way into his heart. Wilf had never felt toward a woman like he felt toward her, and it seemed as though she was feeling the same. Only, there was no way he could pursue a relationship with her, not if he were going to be true and faithful to the one from whom his mother's promised "sign" had come—

"A penny for your thoughts."

With a start, Wilf looked up and was almost overwhelmed by the beauty of the woman standing in the doorway of his room. How did she manage that, he wondered? Especially in her dark glasses and baseball cap, which in spite of everything they had been through together, he had never seen her without.

"Morning," he smiled, steeling his mind against her beauty, against—

Kerensa's radiant smile grew even wider. "Actually, Wilford dear, it is afternoon. You must have been sleeping."

"In this place?" Wilf grinned. "Hospitals, I am learning, are not where one goes to rest. Especially with all your staff running around. What is it, just exactly, that they do?"

"Whatever I tell them," Kerensa replied with a mischievous smile.

"Kerensa—"

"Oh, very well. My work is as a social anthropologist, as you know, and my personal office is at the university. There, except for a secretary and a fairly continuous parade of assistants, I work alone. Nearby, in a suite overlooking the Upper Thames, or, as we call it in Oxford, the Isis, I keep a staff of somewhere between fifteen and twenty secretaries, accountants, and other assorted financial wizards. They do the work of shepherding my father's wealth."

Wilf was amazed. "Are you very involved?"

Kerensa's head swivelled back and forth. "Not at all. You see, I am a secret player. I go to that office only rarely, though James Dearborn—the man whom the world thinks is me—is very dear and keeps me thoroughly apprised of everything. It was to two of James' best accountants, by the way, that you gave the boot yesterday afternoon."

"I'm sorry," Wilf grinned wryly. "I won't do it again, I promise. How are you feeling, by the way?"

"First rate, thank you. No permanent damage, obviously. The doctors said your shoulder had been severely dislocated and that there were bone chips as well?"

"Yeah, and it's my luck that it can't be cast! Now I have to wear this miserable body sling for a month. But my ankle's doing better, and the mild concussion those idiot brothers gave me, whichever time they popped me on the head, should be fine in another day or so."

"And Petroc's knife wound?" Kerensa's face looked pained as she mentioned it.

"Oh, yeah, I forgot about that. Six stitches, and other than that, just a long, miserable scratch. What upsets me most is that the jerk ruined my new jacket!"

"Well," Kerensa giggled, "better the jacket than you. Any stitches in your head?"

"Yeah, two or three in each of the wounds. I forgot about them, too."

"That's because you can't see yourself. Neither would I recommend it. Do you mind awfully if I come in for a chat?"

Wilf shook his head. "Not if you'll tell me how you manage to sound so British even though you aren't."

"Practice," Kerensa sighed as she sat down beside the bed. "Now I have a question for you."

"Shoot."

"How long are you intending to remain in England?"

"Well, I told you I'd give you a week. By the time I get out of here, the week will be up, so my plan is to fly home as soon as I'm released. Why do you ask?" Wilf grinned. "Do you still need a driver?"

"Yes. No, at least not exactly." Now the woman's countenance became troubled. "This may sound terribly forward of me, Wilford, but I very much want you to stay."

"Kerensa, please—"

"With all my heart I mean that! Oh, I know you're thinking of your past and wondering if anyone can find you appealing. That's at least part of the reason why you haven't allowed yourself emotional closeness with other women, and both of us know it. However, you must surely know by now that I find you more than just appealing, and I can quite easily explain why.

"You see, there's something reassuring about a person who stands for something and knows exactly what he stands for. Moreover, when a man is true to himself and to the virtues and values he has personally adopted, as you are, it is not difficult for him to be true to others, most especially the woman he loves. That alone, Wilford, draws my heart and soul to you in ways that I cannot even begin to describe! And it is only one of the things that makes you so attractive. That is why it...it breaks my heart to think that you intend leaving me behind."

"Kerensa, you don't understand!"

"Then help me, dear Wilford. Please help me—"

With a sigh, Wilf gently took Kerensa by the hand, and was acutely aware of the soft feel of her skin. "There's just such a difference between us," he explained, doing his best to ignore his suddenly pounding heart. "Culture, status, education, money—I think the only thing we have in common, besides our shared experience here in Cornwall, is a value system that seems mostly the same."

"Mostly is being far too generous, I am afraid."

"I...don't understand. You told me—"

Gently, Kerensa laid her finger on Wilf's lips, silencing him. "I am an extremely private person, Wilford; I've been forced to be. That's my excuse, I suppose, for not being forthright with you."

"You've lied to me?"

"Well, yes, in a roundabout way. Actually, it's more that I haven't told you everything. Only, it...is just so very difficult to discuss!"

As she lifted her finger from his lips, Kerensa's grip on Wilf's hand tightened perceptibly.

"Like you with Missy, dear Wilford, I, too, helped cause the death of my sister! Now, before you jump to my defense, please allow me to explain. While I may have stopped corresponding with her, from time to time she continued to write me, and for years I have concealed that fact—from you and everyone else that might possibly matter. The truth is that I read her letters, every one of them, even though I didn't respond."

"Why not?"

"I...I don't know. Or perhaps I do, but have never wanted to admit it. Are you absolutely certain you wish to hear this?"

"Only if you want me to," Wilf replied tenderly. "Besides, it is you who is trying to be forthcoming, I believe is how you put it."

"Quite right." Kerensa sighed nervously. "Very well. Partly I failed to respond because I was ashamed of how she was living. The immaturity I think I mentioned. The other part, I suppose, is that she was going blind—"

"The same disease you have?"

For a moment Kerensa hesitated. "Pretty much," she finally sighed. "And frankly, I didn't want to be seen with her."

"Your blindnesss hadn't started yet, I take it?"

Slowly Kerensa shook her head. "No. And maybe I even felt guilt about that. In fact, I'm certain I did. No matter, I didn't want her around, so I ignored her. Then one day when I was pushing to finish my graduation requirements at Princeton—I was eighteen at the time and was due to obtain my bachelor's degree shortly— she sent me another letter. I hadn't heard from her in at least a year, and suddenly she'd concocted this terrible scheme to hold a reunion with me. Without even asking if I was interested or able to come, she laid out her plans and gave me traveling instructions."

Pausing, Kerensa took a deep breath. "Quite naturally, or so it seemed at the time, I resisted, giving myself two reasons. First, I did not want to interrupt my scheduled graduation, even for a few months. And second, I was not about to appear publicly with my sister when she was in such a pitiable state!"

"So, you didn't go." Again Wilf found himself wishing he could see into Kerensa's eyes. "Your sister did, however, and— well, what do you know! No wonder you understood me so well! That was when she died, wasn't it? And now the guilt of it is eating you alive!"

"Y...yes," Kerensa breathed, as sudden tears streamed from under her glasses. "Oh, Wilford! If only I had gone to meet her! If only I had written, even just to turn her down. But I did neither, and now I...I can't stop thinking about it! What if she was murdered simply because she was alone and vulnerable? Or worse, what if she actually did die of a broken heart? Or what if, in despair and loneliness, she took her own life? It now seems obvious that with almost no effort I could have stopped it! Now, every lonely young girl I meet brings tears; every restless spirit I hear about, becomes...becomes— oh, my dear Wilford, how can I stop thinking that I should have...have helped?"

As Kerensa struggled to regain control, her grip on Wilf's hand tightened even more. For a moment, it seemed as though she had no one else in the world to cling to, and Wilf found himself being drawn into—

But no! his mind screamed at him. This could not be, not when he had shared such a precious communication with the girl at the crossing! Surely that was the magical moment Clive and Ann had spoken of and that his mother had promised him, the instantaneous knowledge he now knew was a gift from heaven—that he had found his true companion.

Well, he *had* found her! Not Kerensa Tansin, he forcefully reminded himself but the girl at the crossing! Only—

"Anyway, Wilford darling, I...I dearly wish you would stay."

Almost groaning, Wilf pulled back his hand. "In a major way, so do I, Kerensa," he replied, wanting desperately to think of something else to say, something besides the brutal truth. "But I...I don't think I have the same feelings as you—" Abruptly he forced a grin. "Besides, with an old fiddlefoot like me, there're always other places to go, other people to see."

For a long moment Kerensa gazed straight at him, and Wilf had the uncomfortable sensation that despite her blindness she was seeing right through him.

"There...there's someone else, isn't there," she finally breathed. "Another woman, I mean."

Bleakly Wilf nodded, forgetting altogether that Kerensa couldn't see.

"Wilford?"

"Righto, Dr. Ren," he replied, still hoping he could lighten the moment with a little levity. "I do believe you've sussed it out just right."

"She's very lucky," Kerensa stated quietly, apparently not even noticing Wilf's effort to sound British.

"It may turn out that you're right," he grinned wryly. "I mean, it may not work out, which would probably be lucky for her."

Kerensa's face stiffened. "Please don't say that, Wilford! It will work out; it must! You're the sort of man who has the integrity to make it happen. And when it does, she will be a very lucky woman!"

"I hope so," Wilf grumbled, "though how a person is supposed to chase down the ghost of Morwenna Miller, is beyond me—

"Kerensa, what is it? What's wrong?"

"Morwenna Miller?" Kerensa whispered, her face betraying her confusion. "You're looking for...her ghost?"

Wilf sighed heavily, wishing once again that he'd kept his big mouth shut, but knowing it was too late to avoid saying more. "Yeah, her ghost or spirit or whatever the heck she turns out to be!"

"But...how can this be? Why her? I thought—"

"Believe me, Kerensa, it doesn't do any good to dig into this, for the more one digs, the less sense it makes. Because it's you, though, here are the basics. I saw her at the railroad crossing near where I first met you, the evening before, actually. In fact Clive, Ann, and I all saw her from the train. As our eyes met something amazing passed between us—a wonderful sort of communication concerning us that my mother promised would one day happen.

"Well, Mom was right, and it did! Only now, when I look for her to confirm it, I can't find her; when I see her accidentally, I can't get her to answer me before she vanishes; my only dream about her turned into a nightmare; the Good Lord sent her in answer to my prayer in the smugglers' cave; Daisy Pencarrow has been impersonating her all over the countryside; and...and—"

Startled by the open-mouthed, almost terrified expression on Kerensa's face, Wilf stopped. "Ahh, never mind, Kerensa! I'm sorry to have upset you; really I am! I know it all sounds crazy, but ghost or not, I have no choice but to stay true to that incredible feeling I was given—to stay true to Morwenna Miller."

With a deep, wracking sob, Kerensa rose and fled from the room, and once again Wilf was left to himself. Only this time, instead of pondering, he found himself silently cursing, condemning every tragic moment in his life that had conspired to drive away this dearly loved and more than lovely social anthropologist who had somehow found his heart.

Chapter Twenty-Seven

"Wilford, dear, we're going to miss you terribly!"

Wilf and the Paynes were standing at the tiny railroad station in Looe. It was early morning, wisps of mist lingered in the still air, and a flock of gulls raised a raucous cry out in the ancient harbor. Because the tide was in, both fishing and pleasure craft were heading out into the Channel, their engines throttled down and muted until they had passed the breakwater. On the steel tracks the single-coach train stood ready, the engine throbbing idly as the engineer and elderly conductor conferred over some last-minute business. The setting was incredibly idyllic and peaceful, and Wilf found himself wondering if he would ever see such a sight again.

Smiling wistfully, he reached out and gave Ann a huge, one-armed bear-hug. "Thanks, Ann. You and Clive have been incredible! I only wish I hadn't burdened you with the last few days of my recuperation."

"So do we, for it was terrible of you, just terrible!"

"Clive, that isn't true and you know it!"

"Perhaps you are right, my dear, but I don't wish him to know it. I'd rather have him planning a different sort of itinerary for his next visit." Clive smiled. "On that highly anticipated occasion, my dear American friend, content yourself with being a tourist. No more of this dangerous hero stuff, which is wisely left to us nearly extinct professionals."

"You have my word on it," Wilf chuckled.

"Wonderful, for we have so many exciting places to visit! Tintagel of King Arthur fame; St. Ives with its artist colony; Daphne Du Maurier's Jamaica Inn on Bodmin Moor where the old smugglers gathered; the Hurlers and other neolithic stone circles and quoits; Lanhydrock and Helston and other incredible gardens—well, Wilford, there's no end to things you didn't see! Give us a month, perhaps two, and you can be certain we'll show you a proper Cornwall. England, too, if you're of a mind to see it all."

Wilf laughed easily. "Oh, I'm of a mind, Clive. You can bet on it! And don't worry, either one of you. I'll be planning my return long before you wish to see me. I love Arizona and can't wait to get back, but still, there's something magical about this ancient land—"

"Wilford, do you see who's come to see you off?"

Turning in the direction Ann was looking, Wilf was surprised to see Dr. Kerensa Tansin standing off the verge of the railway near a spectacular clump of flowering hydrangeas.

"Well, what do you know!" he smiled, wondering meanwhile at the catch that had come into his chest and throat—the painful feeling that he would now be forced to officially tell this beautiful woman goodbye. "I haven't seen her since the hospital."

"We know," Ann said quietly. "Nor spoken of her, either—more's the pity."

"Ann, are you playing matchmaker, by any chance?"

"She wouldn't have to," Clive growled, "if you had any sense inside that thick skull of yours. It's no wonder Petroc and his brother couldn't hurt you!"

"No doubt! So, she's here at your invitation, but it's me who has to figure out how to tell her adios? Some friends you've turned out to be."

Clive accepted the gentle rebuke with a look of deep sadness. "No one's forcing you to turn your back on the poor girl, you know. Perhaps with a bit more time—"

"Clive," Wilf pleaded, "of all people, you and Ann should understand! My communication or whatever it was, came with Morwenna Miller, not Kerensa Tansin. Both of you told me that to have peace in this life and the next, I had to be absolutely true to my chosen mate, whether or not I had met her, I believe you said. Well, I don't know when or even if I'll meet Miss Miller, but to be true to everything my mother so carefully crafted within me, I have no choice but to honor that divinely-sent communication and wait!"

Bleakly Wilf smiled. "Now, dear friends, if you'll excuse me for a moment—"

"Don't hurry on our account," Clive grinned wickedly and with no sign of remorse for inviting Kerensa to the station. "Besides, my dear boy, we've nothing more to say to you—"

Good grief, Wilf thought as he limped away, since when had Clive and Ann turned into hopeless old romantics? And why had Kerensa come, anyway? She should have known better! He'd certainly made it plain enough, so why hadn't she left it alone? Why hadn't she just stayed with her work, instead of coming all the way to Cornwall to put them both through this?

But at least, he thought with some relief, she hadn't gone to the trouble of dressing up for him. Same modest field clothing and hiking boots, same wrap-around dark glasses to protect her eyes, same baseball cap. Wilf's smile widened as he gazed at her. She really was an incredible woman! As Clive would put it, so sweet and lovely.

"Morning, Dr. Ren," he grinned as he approached her. "This is a pleasant surprise."

"Do you mean that?" Kerensa asked pointedly. Then she smiled—that same radiant, orthodontically-improved smile Wilf had first noted about her—and instantly the barb was gone from her question. "I expected you to have forgotten me entirely."

"Not hardly."

"Your ankle seems to be doing better. Is your shoulder improving properly?"

"We'll find out in another couple of weeks, I guess."

"Yes, I'm certain." Abruptly Kerensa sobered. "Have you been...successful in your quest?"

"I haven't seen any ghosts, if that's what you mean."

Kerensa nodded. "It is, at least partially. But if you didn't find a ghost, did you...did you at least find the girl? The one you thought might be Morwenna Miller?"

"I did not," Wilf replied with a shake of his head. "I guess I've been too busy lying around the Granite Henge pool, being lazy. Too bad you didn't stay. It might have been... interesting."

"That's a carefully chosen word."

"Isn't it."

For a moment, there was an awkward silence, as though neither knew what to say. Finally, though, Kerensa spoke.

"I apologize if it seems that I am pestering you about Morwenna Miller, Wilford, but I...I feel that I must know. Why do you suppose you have never been able to find her?"

Suddenly Wilf felt tired again—utterly and completely worn out. Besides the terrific beating his body had taken, he was so eternally tired of this Morwenna Miller nonsense—

"Kerensa," he sighed again, "enough with the questions. Okay?"

"Wilford, I am so terribly sorry—" Suddenly Kerensa's lips began to tremble, and Wilf could see that she was on the verge of tears. "Please?" she finally whispered as she struggled to regain control of her emotions. "Please tell me—"

"Oh, for crying out loud!" Wilf grumbled in frustration. "Okay, lady, here it is. I suppose I didn't find her because I stopped looking! Not only do I not know what she is—girl, woman, ghost, spirit, fog, fantasy, or what—but I don't think I want to know. Not any more! The price of knowing is just too doggone high! Besides, with my luck it'll probably turn out that she's nothing more than bad pizza or hallucinations brought on by complete and utter exhaustion!"

"But...I thought...you wanted to find her!"

"No, I *needed* to! Or at least I thought I did." Turning, Wilf glanced back at the station, forcing a smile at Clive and Ann. "Anymore though, I don't even care!"

Carefully, Kerensa looked up at him. "So you'll simply leave England, never knowing?"

"What choice do I have? You tell me!"

In spite of her tears, Kerensa still managed her infuriatingly sweet smile. "You could keep looking."

Wilf laughed harshly. "No, Kerensa, I can't! I'm going home! Today!"

This was interesting, he found himself thinking. Suddenly it felt like Kerensa Tansin was getting pushy, and if there was one trait he had never been able to abide in a woman, it was pushiness! "Besides," and he knew this would be a vicious jab, "didn't I tell you about my budgetary constraints? You might not be able to understand that, but—"

"Wilford," Kerensa responded, placing her hand on his arm and ignoring altogether his reference to her wealth, "this feeling or communication that passed between the two of you that day at the crossing—did you find it exhilarating, filling you with an amazing sense of ecstacy?"

"Kerensa, I don't have time for this. The conductor is getting ready to board the train, and I still have to say goodbye to Clive and Ann."

"Please, Wilford, humor me for just another moment?"

"Oh, for—you know, it's a good thing you're so confounded beautiful. Otherwise, you'd never get away with such brashness!"

"I...I'm sorry, Wilford. Please?"

"Yeah," Wilf sighed with resignation, "that's a good description."

Kerensa smiled sweetly. "Thank you. Was it an almost sacred feeling, overwhelming in a way such as you've never before felt?"

"Yes, it was," Wilford responded, his voice mirroring his exhaustion and frustration.

"And finally," Kerensa concluded, "did it feel as though you had somehow come home? As though your life-long search was over and that you would never be lonely again?"

Startled, Wilf looked down at the lovely woman. "Have you been speaking with Clive or Ann?" he asked narrowly.

"I have," Kerensa replied, "mostly before I returned to Oxford. But we've never spoken of this."

"Then, how did you know how I—"

"I've been describing how *I* felt, Wilford, that day near the pub when you accused me of immodesty. In the very instant when I first heard your voice, even though I was inside the pub at the time, the most overwhelming feeling came over me, and I knew with wonderful certainty that you and I—"

"Kerensa," Wilf pleaded, stopping her by placing his finger against her lips, just as she had done to him in the hospital. "Don't do this! Please. I can't...neither of us can—"

"Because of Morwenna Miller, I believe you said?"

"Yeah," Wilf replied miserably, "Morwenna Miller, or whomever she might someday turn out to be."

For another long moment, silence held between them, neither of the two knowing what else there was to say.

"All aboard!" the old conductor suddenly yelled from near the waiting train. "All aboard for Sandplace, Causeland, St. Keyne, and Liskeard! All aboard!"

"Well," Wilf breathed, feeling worse than ever, "I guess I'd better go."

Earnestly Kerensa took Wilf's free hand. "You cannot leave until I've finished, Wilford. You see, I know the identity of Morwenna Miller!"

"So do I. She's a girl who died ten years ago, at the crossing near Terras Bridge."

"Yes, but I know who she is today, Wilford! Rather, I know who you've been seeing! For days this is all I've thought about, and you must allow me to explain!"

"You'd better hurry, then, because I won't miss that train, Morwenna Miller or not!"

"Very well." Kerensa's actions were now agitated, a fact Wilf could not help but note. "Remember me telling you how I worked? In every way possible I take upon myself the exact characteristics of those I am studying—their dress, their mannerisms, as much as possible even their physical characteristics. If I don't, or for some reason get distracted and stop acting out some part of their lives before I am finished, then I lose everything!"

"Yeah, I remember."

"Good. Here in Cornwall, I have been acting the part of Morwenna Miller."

Wilf was stunned. "You're saying that's who your work has been about?"

"Yes, darling. More importantly, I know without doubt it was me you saw that evening at the crossing!"

"You?" Wilf was flabbergasted! No, *angry* would have been a better description! It was amazing the lengths to which this woman was now going in her effort to keep him in England. "I'm sorry, Kerensa, but this doesn't wash. In America that means I don't believe you! This is all too—well, too convenient. Besides, Morwenna Miller wasn't blind."

"Actually, she was," Kerensa responded sweetly. "But I'm not."

"What? But you...your glasses! You said—"

"It's a part of my work, Wilford. Remember, in every way I had to be like her."

"But she...you weren't wearing glasses at the crossing—"

"She hated to wear them in public, so on public occasions, such as at the crossing where she perished, I followed suit. Incidentally, that was also why I was dressed so shamefully when you saw me the next day at the pub. Except for those times when she wore her school uniform, Morwenna thoroughly enjoyed running around half starkers—half naked, I mean."

Totally perplexed, Wilf rolled his eyes. "Kerensa, can you hear yourself? Can you hear how preposterous all this sounds?"

"Wilford, in spite of how terribly difficult this is for me, I'm doing my best to tell you the truth—"

"Truth?" Wilf laughed harshly. "I don't think you'd recognize truth if it walked up and smacked you in the face! I mean, think of all the lies you've been telling me! You lied to me in the tower and admitted to it in the hospital! Now you admit to lying about being blind, all the while claiming that it wasn't lying at all. You are also claiming to have played the part of

Morwenna Miller just like Daisy did, only for you it was legitimate work and not the fraud she's been charged with. And now you're telling me you never were immodest, but that what you were wearing was the fault of a long-dead girl! I'm telling you, I don't know what to think anymore! Why, Kerensa?"

"Why have I been endeavoring to learn about Morwenna Miller?" Kerensa smiled softly, apparently unfazed by Wilf's accusations. "Remember how Petroc and his cohorts in crime had been trying to stir up Morwenna Miller's relatives so they could extort money from them? And remember how, when no relatives appeared, they kidnaped me instead? Well, my dear Wilford, in an amazingly ironic twist of fate, and though not one of them came close to sussing it out, their little scheme worked better than they thought."

"What?"

"When the supposed appearances of Morwenna Miller's troubled ghost began hitting the tabloids last winter, I decided it was high time I come here to Cornwall, find her using the limited gifts God seems to have given me, and do whatever I possibly could to give the poor child some well-deserved peace. Sadly, for two weeks I, too, had been unsuccessful, and then you came along with your magical communication to thoroughly distract my mind—"

"For crying out loud, Kerensa—"

"You see, Wilford," the social anthropologist interrupted earnestly, "my full name is Kerensa Tansin Miller, though I haven't used my sur-name since my father married that awful woman I told you of. Morwenna Jennepher Miller was my younger sister."

"Oh, come on!" Wilf scorned. "Is this another lie? Surely you can do better than this!"

Kerensa hesitated, breathing deeply, obviously stung by Wilf's last words. "Very well, I'll see if I can satisfy you with a few more ugly details. Rory—"

"Who?"

"I'm sorry. Rory was the name I gave Morwenna when she was born. I don't believe I ever called her anything else. She came here to Cornwall on holiday following the passing of her 'A' levels—the holiday and grand reunion she had planned for us, that I refused to attend?"

"Yeah, I remember your story. Why Cornwall?"

"Because here is where our family's troubles started," Kerensa replied patiently. "At the old mill in Kilminorth Wood. Didn't I mention that to you? Our great-great-grandfather was a smuggler who betrayed his neighbors to the Crown and its Preventive Men. They caught up with the smugglers one stormy night at sea and killed one Robert Mark. Enraged, Mark's neighbors murdered my ancestor, after which his family fled, eventually ending up in America. But tragedy stalked them down through the years, one after another, until finally the Miller's Curse, as it was called by some in our family, caught up with our mother, our father, and then Rory.

"To be honest I thought little of it, Wilford, refusing to believe in curses and scorning those who did. But Rory was obsessed with the idea, literally terrified of it! Then she went blind, and I knew when she met me again she would trumpet, 'I told you so! You're next, Kerensa!' That is the real reason why I didn't meet her here in Cornwall. I couldn't bear thinking that she might be right!"

"But, you were American," Wilf persisted, now caught up in the tale in spite of himself. "Jeanette Fellick said Morwenna Miller was British!"

"My boarding school may have been in America, my dear, but hers was here in England, up in the Lake District. You see, Father and his wife had separated us in every way they could! Rory wrote that she would be wearing her school uniform when I saw her from the train at Terras Bridge, and I believe that's why she never wore anything else when she was there. She knew the hour because of the train's schedule, of course, but because I hadn't written, she never knew what day I might arrive. That was also why she went every afternoon to the crossing, where she...she—"

Kerensa took a deep breath, steeling herself. "Anyway, Wilford, that's why I came here—not to meet you but to try and suss out if Rory had taken her own life as the tabloids reported. And also, to do what little I could to ease the pain of her troubled soul."

"It wasn't suicide," Wilf declared woodenly, no longer certain why he was explaining anything to this woman. "It was an accident. I saw it—in a dream. She lost her balance and fell, and that was all there was to it."

"You saw Rory's death in a dream? But—"

"Wait a minute!" For some reason, Wilf found himself still wanting to believe her. "First things first. You really are claiming it was you outside the train at the crossing?"

Kerensa's lovely countenance grew very serious. "Yes, darling, it was me."

"Why didn't you say something?"

"When? If you will remember, there was a train window between us. Besides, I couldn't speak with you when I was acting Rory's part—not and accomplish what I so desperately wanted to accomplish. As it turned out, however, my concentration was ruined anyway."

"Because of that 'magical communication' you felt!"

Kerensa nodded. "Yes. In the very instant I saw you, it was ruined! You have spoken of the wonderful communication you had with she whom you thought was Rory? Wilford, darling, I also experienced it that evening—at the very same time and in the very same place! And from that moment I could think of nothing else!"

"Come on, Kerensa!" Now Wilf literally threw his hands into the air. "A moment ago you said it happened to you at the pub—*The Copley Arms*—and now you say it was at the crossing! That's another lie, doggone it!"

Kerensa's smile couldn't have been sweeter. "No, darling, it isn't. In actuality, our glorious communication with each other happened every time I either saw you, which was when I wasn't wearing these terrible blinders, or when I heard your voice! It was completely distracting, of course, but absolutely sweet and wonderful! Now, like my pain over my poor sister's death, I can't seem to make it go away—"

"If this is all true," Wilf interrupted, his skepticism now running rampant, "surely you could have said something that day in the tower, or later in the hospital, when I told you what I was struggling with."

Kerensa laughed, and to Wilf it still had the sound like the tinkling of fine crystal. "Truthfully, Wilford, in the tower when we met Daisy, I was too surprised to say anything. I had no idea you would know of Morwenna Miller. Then after we spoke in the hospital and I realized you had felt the same glorious communication from me that I had felt from you, I became terrified that if I told you it was me instead of Rory at the crossing, you would think me daft, or worse, a liar—a conniving single woman who would do or say anything to trap a man, particularly a wonderful man such as yourself."

"And you aren't those things?" Wilf forced a grin, though he no longer much cared if he wounded the feelings of this incredibly beautiful liar.

"Not unless I must be." Kerensa smiled in return, her countenance radiating perfect sincerity. "Remember, my dear, I was cherishing those wonderful feelings as much as you, doing all I could to be near you at every possible moment, and wondering all the while why you showed no reciprocal interest in me. Then when you told me, I...I...couldn't see a way through! That is why I ran from your hospital room, Wilford, why I returned to Oxford that very day!"

"Right." Wilf shook his head in utter perplexity. "Well, I...I don't know what to say, Kerensa. I...don't even know what to think! All along I believed I was helping a blind woman—"

"I am blind when I am wearing these glasses." Kerensa reached up and tapped the darkened lenses with her finger. "And when I was standing at the crossing the evening you came through, Wilford, and even the next day at the pub, I was as much my sister as I knew how to be. Yet still it was me who saw you through the train window, and in that instant I was consumed with the most wonderful and overwhelming sense of love and belonging I have ever felt! Please, my darling! Please? You must believe me—"

"Maybe in time, Kerensa. I'll just have to wait and see. For now, though, Clive and Ann are waiting, so I...uh—

"Ahh, this is no good! I can't leave it this way! Mom used to tell us not only to be scrupulously honest, but that only cowards avoided the painful side of truth.

"So," Wilf continued as he took a deep breath, "you've proven yourself a poor but lovely liar, Dr. Ren. Thank you for what you're offering, but no thanks! You have a good life, you hear? Maybe I'll see you around."

And with a great and terrible sadness engulfing his soul, Wilf turned and limped slowly away.

Well, that's pretty much the story Wilf told. Despite the fact that he'd hardly dated at all in ten years, in less than two weeks in Cornwall he'd somehow managed to fall into—and back out of—love with both a lovely ghost he could never find and an incredibly beautiful but conniving and untruthful social anthropologist. For a fact, he said, he was no longer even sure of the latter woman's professional claims. After all, he'd never read anything by a Dr. Kerensa Tansin! Yes, sir, harsh experience had taught Wilf Abbott not to believe anything about either woman that he couldn't see, hear, touch, taste or feel for himself....

Chapter Twenty-Eight

"Wilford," Kerensa smiled as sweetly as she possibly could, though she was smiling and speaking only to his retreating back, "one more thing before you go."

"Yes, Kerensa," Wilf almost groaned as he forced himself to turn around.

"I was wondering," Kerensa asked as she stepped toward him, her hand holding the bill of her baseball cap, "did the hair of the girl you saw at the crossing, look perhaps a little like mine?" Quickly she lifted the hat and, with a shake of her head, sent her dark hair tumbling and cascading down over her shoulders.

"I...uh—"

"And was she dressed in a school uniform similar to this one?"

Wilf could only stare as Kerensa pulled from her ever-present pack a navy blazer, white blouse and gray skirt.

"And...when you looked into her eyes, Wilford, were they in color, something like mine?"

Carefully Kerensa removed the darkly tinted, wrap-around glasses, and in that same instant Wilf found himself gazing down into the deep, liquid blueness of the most beautiful eyes he had ever seen—the same incredible eyes he had seen gazing up at him the evening he had first passed through the fateful crossing at Terras Bridge!

More, his entire being was in that same instant filled with a most incredible sensation—the same overwhelming and glorious communication he had cherished every time he had looked into those amazing eyes since then—

"It...it *was* you!"

"I know, my darling," Kerensa replied as she took Wilf's hand in both of hers. "That's what I have been trying to find a way to tell you for two horrible but wonderful weeks."

Wilf was now shaking his head, trying to come to grips with this amazing new reality. She hadn't been lying! All along, the beautiful Kerensa Tansin—no, Kerensa Tansin *Miller*—had been telling the truth! It had been she at the crossing, she who had filled his soul with the joyous promise that she was to be his life, his happiness, his peace! She truly was the one who would be the fulfilment of his mother's promise! It was she who was to be his eternal home!

"I...love you!" he breathed, feeling not in the least uncomfortable with the words that had formed in his mouth.

"And I love you, my darling."

Wilf smiled down at her. "How...do you do it?"

"Do what?"

"Oh, I don't know. Look so beautiful, I guess. No, it's more than that. How do you be you? Every part of you is so overwhelmingly attractive to me, so vitally necessary, actually, that I...I...Well, I guess that's what I'm talking about. How do you be you?"

Kerensa laughed, and again Wilf was awed by the sound of it. "I don't know, Wilford. How is it that you cause me to feel a little dizzy, or light-headed, as though I'm floating on clouds when I touch you or hear your voice or see the tender goodness in your eyes?"

"I do that?"

"Always!"

Wilf grinned crookedly. "Beats me, Kerensa".

Wilf was now serious. But promise me something "Please

don't ever vanish or disappear on me again."

"You have my word, Wilford dear."

Wilf regarded Kerensa quizzically. "Thank you. But you seemed to do it so easily. Tell me, that second night at the crossing, when we saw each other just before the train passed between us—how did you manage to disappear so quickly? Did you grab hold of the train, find a hiding place, or what?"

"Beats me," Kerensa smiled sweetly, mimicking Wilf's too-frequent laconic reply. "Perhaps it is you who are more blind than you think."

"Yeah, right." Carefully Wilf searched Kerensa's lovely countenance. "You aren't going to tell me, are you."

"Well," the social anthropologist's smile continued, "if I'm to keep you around for the rest of forever, darling, then of course I must maintain at least some sense of mystery."

"All right," Wilf capitulated with a sigh. "Keep your weird little secret. But at least you can tell me why you didn't speak with me that evening after I had broken your concentration, or earlier that same morning, outside the pasty shop in Polperro. I saw you in both those places, Kerensa, and I *know* you saw me. Why didn't you—"

"The pasty shop in Polperro?" Kerensa questioned softly, looking confused. "I've never been near a pasty shop in Polperro."

"But, I saw you there, though I admit it was pretty misty. I saw you standing just outside the window. I know it was you, for I could see your face clearly! You saw me, too! I could even feel—

"Wait a minute!" Now Wilf's eyes opened wide. "If it wasn't you, and Daisy told us flat-out it wasn't her, then…oh, no! Don't tell me I've actually seen your sister's spirit!"

For a moment Kerensa gazed up into Wilf's face, her startlingly blue eyes dancing with merriment. Suddenly, and completely unexpectedly, she winked.

"Gotcha!" she said with a wide, sweet smile, sounding very American as she said it. And Wilf could do nothing but wrap his one good arm around her amazingly tiny waist, squeezing her close and reveling in the feel of her arms encircling his neck and drawing herself even closer.

"Don't you ever do that again!" he scolded, finally releasing her at least a little and pushing the laughter from his voice. "But I do have one question about your effective little vanishing act, Kerensa—one that needs an honest answer. I'll even say please, because this one I have found troubling. After you showed me those steps leading up out of the old smugglers' cave, how did you manage to disappear so quickly? Or get in there to show them to me in the first place? Did Neville let you out of the stocks for a few moments? And how did you know about that old trap door at the top of the tunnel, or get it closed with the dust back around its edges after you climbed back out—"

Arrested by the completely bewildered expression on Kerensa's lovely face, Wilf stopped. "Kerensa? I don't like that look."

"I...I don't mean to frighten you." The woman pressed against him was deathly serious, and Wilf could easily sense her sincerity. "Nevertheless, darling, I have absolutely no idea what you are talking about!"

For a moment and then another Wilf searched Kerensa's eyes, knowing as he searched that there would be no real surprises found there—ever. Then his voice lowered perceptibly. "It...wasn't you at all, was it."

It was a statement Wilf had made, not a question, and in that same instant, both he and Kerensa knew the truth of what had happened. He *had* seen Morwenna Miller. Somehow she had been sent, at his prayerful and specific request, to aid him in delivering from evil her beloved older sister.

"Oh, glory!" Wilf breathed. "That's something we'd better not tell anyone! Ever!"

"Not at least until we have a dozen grandchildren." The lovely Kerensa was standing pressed against him, her arms still tight around his neck but with her head pulled back and her disconcertingly lovely eyes fastened upon him in a way such as he had never seen—never even imagined! It was all

Wilf could do, at that supernal moment, to think! It was all—

"I...uh...I thought proposing was the man's job," he finally managed.

"Depends on who gets to it first." Kerensa smiled sweetly. "Somewhat like the gifted water at St. Keynes' old well. Besides, Wilford darling, in some things you can be so eternally slow!"

Before Wilf could think of any response at all, new tears started from the amazingly deep blueness of Kerensa's eyes, and quickly she pressed her finger to his lips. "Don't say anything, darling. Just listen, for I must say this, and you must never forget it.

"Wilford Abbott, I...I want you to know that your life-long search is over. Since girlhood I have saved my heart, my soul, every particle of my being, for you alone, and in every way possible the wait has proven worth it! Thank you forever for being the man your precious mother taught her son to become! Whether here or in Arizona or wherever else we may choose for ourselves, you will never be lonely again. That is a solemn vow I now make to you. Welcome home, my dearest!"

"Last call for Liskeard!" the elderly conductor shouted pointedly. "Allll aboarrrd!"

"Hello," Clive said as he clapped his hand on the conductor's bony shoulder. "Nothing quite like young love, what? Looks as though our man Wilford will be missing the train this morning, no matter how loudly you shout!"

"And well he should," Ann added happily as she wiped at her eyes and then winked at the grinning conductor. "Cheerio, my good man! And if you should see us again sometime, don't you be putting up with any more of my husband's cheeky behavior."

"My cheeky behavior?" Clive argued as he took Ann by the arm to lead her away from the already moving train. "That's a lovely thing to say about your sweetheart. Simply lovely! Why don't you treat me like Kerensa there is doing for young Wilford? Now and then *I* could use a little snogging, you know."

"Since when," Ann chuckled as she slid her arm about her husband's waist and guided him toward their old Passat, "could you stop with just a little?"

And Wilf, his lips finally accepting Kerensa's first sweet and eager kiss, was paying not a modicum of attention to either of them.